TOM SAW THE FORM OF A GREAT SHARK LAUNCHED AT
CAPTAIN WESTON.

Page 200.

Tom Swift and His Submarine Boat

TOM SWIFT AND HIS SUBMARINE BOAT

OR

Under the Ocean for Sunken Treasure

BY

VICTOR APPLETON

AUTHOR OF "TOM SWIFT AND HIS MOTOR-CYCLE," "TOM SWIFT AND HIS MOTOR-BOAT," ETC.

ILLUSTRATED

NEW YORK
GROSSET & DUNLAP
PUBLISHERS

CONTENTS

iii

iv CONTENTS

TOM SWIFT AND HIS SUBMARINE BOAT

CHAPTER I

NEWS OF A TREASURE WRECK

THERE was a rushing, whizzing, throbbing noise in the air. A great body, like that of some immense bird, sailed along, casting a grotesque shadow on the ground below. An elderly man, who was seated on the porch of a large house, started to his feet in alarm.

"Gracious goodness! What was that, Mrs. Baggert?" he called to a motherly-looking woman who stood in the doorway. "What happened?"

"Nothing much, Mr. Swift," was the calm reply. "I think that was Tom and Mr. Sharp in their airship, that's all. I didn't see it, but the noise sounded like that of the *Red Cloud.*"

"Of course! To be sure!" exclaimed Mr. Barton Swift, the well-known inventor, as he started down the path in order to get a good view of the air, unobstructed by the trees. "Yes, there they are," he added. "That's the airship, but I didn't expect them back so soon. They must have made good time from Shopton. I wonder if anything can be the matter that they hurried so?"

He gazed aloft toward where a queerly-shaped machine was circling about nearly five hundred feet in the air, for the craft, after swooping down close to the house, had ascended and was now hovering just above the line of breakers that marked the New Jersey seacoast, where Mr. Swift had taken up a temporary residence.

"Don't begin worrying, Mr. Swift," advised Mrs. Baggert, the housekeeper. "You've got too much to do, if you get that new boat done, to worry."

"That's so. I must not worry. But I wish Tom and Mr. Sharp would land, for I want to talk to them."

As if the occupants of the airship had heard the words of the aged inventor, they headed their craft toward earth. The combined aeroplane and dirigible balloon, a most wonderful traveler of the air, swung around, and then, with the deflection rudders slanted downward, came on with a rush. When near the landing place, just at the side of the house, the motor was stopped, and the gas, with a hissing noise, rushed into the red aluminum container. This immediately made the ship more buoyant and it landed almost as gently as a feather.

No sooner had the wheels which formed the lower part of the craft touched the ground than there leaped from the cabin of the *Red Cloud* a young man.

"Well, dad!" he exclaimed. "Here we are again, safe and sound. Made a record, too. Touched ninety miles an hour at times—didn't we, Mr. Sharp?"

"That's what," agreed a tall, thin, dark-complexioned man, who followed Tom Swift more leisurely in his exit from the cabin. Mr. Sharp, a veteran aeronaut, stopped to fasten guy ropes from the airship to strong stakes driven into the ground.

"And we'd have done better, only we struck a hard wind against us about two miles up in the air, which delayed us," went on Tom. "Did you hear us coming, dad?"

"Yes, and it startled him," put in Mrs. Baggert. "I guess he wasn't expecting you."

"Oh, well, I shouldn't have been so alarmed, only I was thinking deeply about a certain change I am going to make in the submarine, Tom. I was day-dreaming, I think, when your ship whizzed through the air. But tell me, did you find everything all right at Shopton? No signs of any of those scoundrels of the Happy Harry gang having been around?" and Mr. Swift looked anxiously at his son.

"Not a sign, dad," replied Tom quickly. "Everything was all right. We brought the things you wanted. They're in the airship. Oh, but it was a fine trip. I'd like to take another right out to sea."

"Not now, Tom," said his father. "I want you to help me. And I need Mr. Sharp's help, too. Get the things out of the car, and we'll go to the shop."

"First I think we'd better put the airship away," advised Mr. Sharp. "I don't just like the looks of the weather, and, besides, if we leave the ship exposed we'll be sure to have a crowd around sooner or later, and we don't want that."

"No, indeed," remarked the aged inventor hastily. "I don't want people prying around the submarine shed. By all means put the airship away, and then come into the shop."

In spite of its great size the aeroplane was easily wheeled along by Tom and Mr. Sharp, for the gas in the container made it so buoyant that it barely touched the earth. A little more of the powerful vapor and the *Red Cloud* would have risen by itself. In a few minutes the wonderful craft, of which my readers have been told in detail in a previous volume, was safely housed in a large tent, which was securely fastened.

Mr. Sharp and Tom, carrying some bundles which they had taken from the car, or cabin, of the craft, went toward a large shed, which adjoined the house that Mr. Swift had hired for the season at the seashore. They found the lad's father standing before a great shape, which loomed up dimly in the semi-darkness of the building. It was like an immense cylinder, pointed at either end, and here and there were openings, covered with thick glass, like immense, bulging eyes. From the number of tools and machinery all about the place, and from the appearance of the great cylinder itself, it was easy to see that it was only partly completed.

"Well, how goes it, dad?" asked the youth, as he deposited his bundle on a bench. "Do you think you can make it work?"

"I think so, Tom. The positive and negative plates are giving me considerable trouble, though. But I guess we can solve the problem. Did you bring me the galvanometer?"

"Yes, and all the other things," and the young

inventor proceeded to take the articles from the bundles he carried.

Mr. Swift looked them over carefully, while Tom walked about examining the submarine, for such was the queer craft that was contained in the shed. He noted that some progress had been made on it since he had left the seacoast several days before to make a trip to Shopton, in New York State, where the Swift home was located, after some tools and apparatus that his father wanted to obtain from his workshop there.

"You and Mr. Jackson have put on several new plates," observed the lad after a pause.

"Yes," admitted his father. "Garret and I weren't idle, were we, Garret?" and he nodded to the aged engineer, who had been in his employ for many years.

"No; and I guess we'll soon have her in the water, Tom, now that you and Mr. Sharp are here to help us," replied Garret Jackson.

"We ought to have Mr. Damon here to bless the submarine and his liver and collar buttons a few times," put in Mr. Sharp, who brought in another bundle. He referred to an eccentric individual who had recently made an airship voyage with himself and Tom, Mr. Damon's peculiarity being to use continually such expressions as: "Bless my soul! Bless my liver!"

"Well, I'll be glad when we can make a trial trip," went on Tom. "I've traveled pretty fast on land with my motor-cycle, and we certainly have hummed through the air. Now I want to see how it feels to scoot along under water."

"Well, if everything goes well we'll be in a position to make a trial trip inside of a month," remarked the aged inventor. "Look here, Mr. Sharp, I made a change in the steering gear, which I'd like you and Tom to consider."

The three walked around to the rear of the odd-looking structure, if an object shaped like a cigar can be said to have a front and rear, and the inventor, his son, and the aeronaut were soon deep in a discussion of the technicalities connected with under-water navigation.

A little later they went into the house, in response to a summons from the supper bell, vigorously rung by Mrs. Baggert. She was not fond of waiting with meals, and even the most serious problem of mechanics was, in her estimation, as nothing compared with having the soup get cold, or the possibility of not having the meat done to a turn.

The meal was interspersed with remarks about the recent airship flight of Tom and Mr. Sharp, and discussions about the new submarine. This talk went on even after the table was cleared off and the three had adjourned to the sitting-room. There Mr. Swift brought out pencil and paper, and soon he and Mr. Sharp were engrossed in calculating the pressure per square inch of sea water at a depth of three miles.

"Do you intend to go as deep as that?" asked Tom, looking up from a paper he was reading.

"Possibly," replied his father; and his son resumed his perusal of the sheet.

"Now," went on the inventor to the aeronaut, "I have another plan. In addition to the positive and negative plates which will form our motive power, I am going to install forward and aft propellers, to use in case of accident——"

"I say, dad! Did you see this?" suddenly exclaimed Tom, getting up from his chair, and holding his finger on a certain place in the page of the paper.

"Did I see what?" asked Mr. Swift.

"Why, this account of the sinking of the treasure ship."

"Treasure ship? No. Where?"

"Listen," went on Tom. "I'll read it: 'Further advices from Montevideo, Uruguay, South America, state that all hope has been given up of recovering the steamship *Boldero,* which foundered and went down off that coast in the recent gale. Not only has all hope been abandoned of raising the vessel, but it is feared that no part of the three hundred thousand dollars in gold bullion which she carried will ever be recovered. Expert divers who were taken to the scene of the wreck state that the depth of water, and the many currents existing there, due to a submerged shoal, preclude any possibility of getting at the hull. The bullion, it is believed, was to have been used to further the interests of a certain revolutionary faction, but it seems likely that they will have to look elsewhere for the sinews of war. Besides the bullion the ship also carried several cases of rifles, it is stated, and other valuable cargo. The crew and what few passengers the *Boldero* carried were, contrary to the first reports, all saved by taking to the boats. It appears that some of the ship's plates were sprung by the stress in which she labored in a storm, and she filled and sank gradually.' There! what do you think of that, dad?" cried Tom as he finished.

"What do I think of it? Why, I think it's too bad for the revolutionists, Tom, of course."

"No; I mean about the treasure being still on board the ship. What about that?"

"Well, it's likely to stay there, if the divers can't get at it. Now, Mr. Sharp, about the propellers——"

"Wait, dad!" cried Tom earnestly.

"Why, Tom, what's the matter?" asked Mr. Swift in some surprise.

"How soon before we can finish our submarine?" went on Tom, not answering the question.

"About a month. Why?"

"Why? Dad, why can't we have a try for that treasure? It ought to be comparatively easy to find that sunken ship off the coast of Uruguay. In our submarine we can get close up to it, and in the new diving suits you invented we can get at that gold bullion. Three hundred thousand dollars! Think of it, dad! Three hundred thousand dollars! We could easily claim all of it, since the owners have abandoned it, but we would be satisfied with half. Let's hurry up, finish the submarine, and have a try for it."

"But, Tom, you forget that I am to enter my new ship in the trials for the prize offered by the United States Government."

"How much is the prize if you win it?" asked Tom.

"Fifty thousand dollars."

"Well, here's a chance to make three times that much at least, and maybe more. Dad, let the Government prize go, and try for the treasure. Will you?"

Tom looked eagerly at his father, his eyes shining with anticipation. Mr. Swift was not a quick thinker, but the idea his son had proposed made an impression on him. He reached out his hand for the paper in which the young inventor had seen the account of the sunken treasure. Slowly he read it through. Then he passed it to Mr. Sharp.

"What do you think of it?" he asked of the aeronaut.

"There's a possibility," remarked the balloonist. "We might try for it. We can easily go three miles down, and it doesn't lie as deeply as that, if this account is true. Yes, we might try for it. But we'd have to omit the Government contests."

"Will you, dad?" asked Tom again.

Mr. Swift considered a moment longer.

"Yes, Tom, I will," he finally decided. "Going after the treasure will be likely to afford us a better test of the submarine than would any Government tests. We'll try to locate the sunken *Boldero*."

"Hurrah!" cried the lad, taking the paper from Mr. Sharp and waving it in the air. "That's the stuff! Now for a search for the submarine treasure!"

CHAPTER II

FINISHING THE SUBMARINE

"WHAT's the matter?" cried Mrs. Baggert, the housekeeper, hurrying in from the kitchen, where she was washing the dishes. "Have you seen some of those scoundrels who robbed you, Mr. Swift? If you have, the police down here ought to——"

"No, it's nothing like that," explained Mr. Swift. "Tom has merely discovered in the paper an account of a sunken treasure ship, and he wants us to go after it, down under the ocean."

"Oh, dear! Some more of Captain Kidd's hidden hoard, I suppose?" ventured the housekeeper. "Don't you bother with it, Mr. Swift. I had a cousin once, and he got set in the notion that he knew where that pirate's treasure was. He spent all the money he had and all he could borrow digging for it, and he never found a penny. Don't waste your time on such foolishness. It's bad enough to be building airships and submarines, without going after treasure." Mrs. Baggert spoke with the freedom of an old friend rather than a hired housekeeper, but she had been in the family ever since Tom's mother died, when he was a baby, and she had many privileges.

"Oh, this isn't any of Kidd's treasure," Tom assured her. "If we get it, Mrs. Baggert, I'll buy you a diamond ring."

"Humph!" she exclaimed, as Tom began to hug her in boyish fashion. "I guess *I'll* have to buy all the diamond rings I want, if I have to depend on your treasure for them," and she went back to the kitchen.

"Well," went on Mr. Swift after a pause, "if we are going into the treasure-hunting business, Tom, we'll have to get right to work. In the first place, we must find out more about this ship, and just where it was sunk."

"I can do that part," said Mr. Sharp. "I know some sea captains, and they can put me on the track of locating the exact spot. In fact, it might not be a bad idea to take an expert navigator with us. I can manage in the air all right, but I confess that working out a location under water is beyond me."

"Yes, an old sea captain wouldn't be a bad idea, by any means," conceded Mr. Swift. "Well, if you'll attend to that detail, Mr. Sharp, Tom,

Mr. Jackson and I will finish the submarine. Most of the work is done, however, and it only remains to install the engine and motors. Now, in regard to the negative and positive electric plates, I'd like your opinion, Tom."

For Tom Swift was an inventor, second in ability only to his father, and his advice was often sought by his parent on matters of electrical construction, for the lad had made a specialty of that branch of science.

While father and son were deep in a discussion of the apparatus of the submarine, there will be an opportunity to make the reader a little better acquainted with them. Those of you who have read the previous volumes of this series do not need to be told who Tom Swift is. Others, however, may be glad to have a proper introduction to him.

Tom Swift lived with his father, Barton Swift, in the village of Shopton, New York. The Swift home was on the outskirts of the town, and the large house was surrounded by a number of machine shops, in which father and son, aided by Garret Jackson, the engineer, did their experimental and constructive work. Their house was not far from Lake Carlopa, a fairly large body of water, on which Tom often speeded his motorboat.

In the first volume of this series, entitled "Tom Swift and His Motor-Cycle," it was told how he became acquainted with Mr. Wakefield Damon, who suffered an accident while riding one of the speedy machines. The accident disgusted Mr. Damon with motor-cycles, and Tom secured it for a low price. He had many adventures on it, chief among which was being knocked senseless and robbed of a valuable patent model belonging to his father, which he was taking to Albany. The attack was committed by a gang known as the Happy Harry gang, who were acting at the instigation of a syndicate of rich men, who wanted to secure control of a certain patent turbine engine which Mr. Swift had invented.

Tom set out in pursuit of the thieves, after recovering from their attack, and had a strenuous time before he located them.

In the second volume, entitled "Tom Swift and His Motor-Boat," there was related our hero's adventures in a fine craft which was recovered from the thieves and sold at auction. There was a mystery connected with the boat, and for a long time Tom could not solve it. He was aided, however, by his chum, Ned Newton, who worked in the Shopton Bank, and also by Mr. Damon and Eradicate Sampson, an aged colored whitewasher, who formed quite an attachment for Tom.

In his motor-boat Tom had more than one race with Andy Foger, a rich lad of Shopton, who was a sort of bully. He had red hair and squinty eyes, and was as mean in character as he was in looks. He and his cronies, Sam Snedecker and Pete Bailey, made trouble for Tom, chiefly because Tom managed to beat Andy twice in boat races.

It was while in his motor-boat, *Arrow,* that Tom formed the acquaintance of John Sharp, a veteran balloonist. While coming down Lake Carlopa on the way to the Swift home, which had been entered by thieves, Tom, his father and Ned Newton, saw a balloon on fire over the lake. Hanging from a trapeze on it was Mr. Sharp, who had made an ascension from a fair ground. By hard work on the part of Tom and his friends the aeronaut was saved, and took up his residence with the Swifts.

His advent was most auspicious, for Tom and his father were then engaged in perfecting an airship, and Mr. Sharp was able to lend them his skill, so that the craft was soon constructed.

In the third volume, called "Tom Swift and His Airship," there was set down the doings of the young inventor, Mr. Sharp and Mr. Damon on a trip above the clouds. They undertook it merely for pleasure, but they encountered considerable danger before they completed it, for they nearly fell into a blazing forest once, and were later fired at by a crowd of excited people. This last act was to effect their capture, for they were taken for a gang of bank robbers, and this was due directly to Andy Foger.

The morning after Tom and his friends started on their trip in the air, the Shopton Bank was found to have been looted of seventy-five thousand dollars. Andy Foger at once told the police that Tom Swift had taken the money, and when asked how he knew this, he said he had seen Tom hanging around the bank the night before the vault was burst open, and that the young inventor had some burglar tools in his possession. Warrants were at once sworn out for Tom and Mr. Damon, who was also accused of being one of the robbers, and a reward of five thousand dollars was offered.

Tom, Mr. Damon and Mr. Sharp sailed on, all unaware of this, and unable to account for being fired upon, until they accidentally read in the paper an account of their supposed misdeeds. They lost no time in starting back home, and on the way got on the track of the real bank robbers, who were members of the Happy Harry gang.

How the robbers were captured in an exciting raid, how Tom recovered most of the stolen money, and how he gave Andy Foger a deserved thrashing for giving a false clue was told of, and there was an account of a race in which the *Red Cloud* (as the airship was called) took part, as well as details of how Tom and his friends secured the reward, which Andy Foger hoped to collect.

Those of you who care to know how the *Red Cloud* was constructed, and how she behaved in the air, even during accidents and when struck by lightning, may learn by reading the third volume, for the airship was one of the most successful ever constructed.

When the craft was finished, and the navigators were ready to start on their first long trip, Mr. Swift was asked to go with them. He declined, but would not tell why, until Tom, pressing him for an answer, learned that his father was planning a submarine boat, which he hoped to enter in some trials for Government prizes. Mr. Swift remained at home to work on this submarine, while his son and Mr. Sharp were sailing above the clouds.

On their return, however, and after the bank mystery had been cleared up, Tom and Mr. Sharp aided Mr. Swift in completing the submarine, until, when the present story opens, it needed but little additional work to make the craft ready for the water.

Of course it had to be built near the sea, as it would have been impossible to transport it overland from Shopton. So, before the keel was laid, Mr. Swift rented a large cottage at a secluded place on the New Jersey coast and there, after erecting a large shed, the work on the. *Advance,* as the under-water ship was called, was begun.

It was soon to be launched in a large creek that extended in from the ocean and had plenty of water at high tide. Tom and Mr. Sharp made several trips back and forth from Shopton in their airship, to see that all was safe at home and occasionally to get needed tools and supplies from the shops, for not all the apparatus could be moved from Shopton to the coast.

It was when returning from one of these trips that Tom brought with him the paper containing an account of the wreck of the *Boldero* and the sinking of the treasure she carried.

Until late that night the three fortune-hunters discussed various matters.

"We'll hurry work on the ship," said Mr. Swift at length. "Tom, I wonder if your friend, Mr. Damon, would care to try how it seems under water? He stood the air trip fairly well."

"I'll write and ask him," answered the lad. "I'm sure he'll go."

Securing, a few days later, the assistance of two mechanics, whom he knew he could trust, for as yet the construction of the *Advance* was a secret, Mr. Swift prepared to rush work on the submarine, and for the next three weeks there were busy times in the shed next to the seaside cottage. So busy, in fact, were Tom and Mr. Sharp, that they only found opportunity for one trip in the airship, and that was to get some supplies from the shops at home.

"Well," remarked Mr. Swift one night, at the close of a hard day's work, "another week will see our craft completed. Then we will put it in the water and see how it floats, and whether it submerges as I hope it does. But come on, Tom. I want to lock up. I'm very tired to-night."

"All right, dad," answered the young inventor, coming from the darkened rear of the shop. "I just want to——"

He paused suddenly, and appeared to be listening. Then he moved softly back to where he had come from.

"What's the matter?" asked his father in a whisper. "What's up, Tom?"

The lad did not answer. Mr. Swift, with a

worried look on his face, followed his son. Mr. Sharp stood in the door of the shop.

"I thought I heard some one moving around back here," went on Tom quietly.

"Some one in this shop!" exclaimed the aged inventor excitedly. "Some one trying to steal my ideas again! Mr. Sharp, come here! Bring that rifle! We'll teach these scoundrels a lesson!"

Tom quickly darted back to the extreme rear of the building. There was a scuffle, and the next minute Tom cried out:

"What are you doing here?"

"Ha! I beg your pardon," replied a voice. "I am looking for Mr. Barton Swift."

"My father," remarked Tom. "But that's a queer place to look for him. He's up front. Father, here's a man who wishes to see you," he called.

"Yes, I strolled in, and seeing no one about I went to the rear of the place," the voice went on. "I hope I haven't transgressed."

"We were busy on the other side of the shop, I guess," replied Tom, and he looked suspiciously at the man who emerged from the darkness into the light from a window. "I beg your pardon for grabbing you the way I did," went on the lad, "but I thought you were one of a gang of men we've been having trouble with."

"Oh, that's all right," continued the man easily. "I know Mr. Swift, and I think he will remember me. Ah, Mr. Swift, how do you do?" he added quickly, catching sight of Tom's father, who, with Mr. Sharp, was coming to meet the lad.

"Addison Berg!" exclaimed the aged inventor as he saw the man's face more plainly. "What are you doing here?"

"I came to see you," replied the man. "May I have a talk with you privately?"

"I—I suppose so," assented Mr. Swift nervously. "Come into the house."

Mr. Berg left Tom's side and advanced to where Mr. Swift was standing. Together the two emerged from the now fast darkening shop and went toward the house.

"Who is he?" asked Mr. Sharp of the young inventor in a whisper.

"I don't know," replied the lad; "but, whoever he is, dad seems afraid of him. I'm going to keep my eyes open."

CHAPTER III

MR. BERG IS ASTONISHED

FOLLOWING his father and the stranger, whom the aged inventor had addressed as Mr. Berg, Tom and Mr. Sharp entered the house, the lad having first made sure that Garret Jackson was on guard in the shop that contained the submarine.

"Now," said Mr. Swift to the newcomer, "I am at your service. What is it you wish?"

"In the first place, let me apologize for having startled you and your friends," began the man. "I had no idea of sneaking into your workshop, but I had just arrived here, and seeing the doors open I went in. I heard no one about, and I wandered to the back of the place. There I happened to stumble over a board——"

"And I heard you," interrupted Tom.

"Is this one of your employes?" asked Mr. Berg in rather frigid tones.

"That is my son," replied Mr. Swift.

23

"Oh, I beg your pardon." The man's manner changed quickly. "Well, I guess you did hear me, young man. I didn't intend to bark my shins the way I did, either. You must have taken me for a burglar or a sneak thief."

"I have been very much bothered by a gang of unscrupulous men," said Mr. Swift, "and I suppose Tom thought it was some of them sneaking around again."

"That's what I did," added the lad. "I wasn't going to have any one steal the secret of the submarine if I could help it."

"Quite right! Quite right!" exclaimed Mr. Berg. "But my purpose was an open one. As you know, Mr. Swift, I represent the firm of Bentley & Eagert, builders of submarine boats and torpedoes. They heard that you were constructing a craft to take part in the competitive prize tests of the United States Government, and they asked me to come and see you to learn when your ship would be ready. Ours is completed, but we recognize that it will be for the best interests of all concerned if there are a number of contestants, and my firm did not want to send in their entry until they knew that you were about finished with your ship. How about it? Are you ready to compete?"

"Yes," said Mr. Swift slowly. "We are about

ready. My craft needs a few finishing touches, and then it will be ready to launch."

"Then we may expect a good contest on your part," suggested Mr. Berg.

"Well," began the aged inventor, "I don't know about that."

"What's that?" exclaimed Mr. Berg.

"I said I wasn't quite sure that we would compete," went on Mr. Swift. "You see, when I first got this idea for a submarine boat I had it in mind to try for the Government prize of fifty thousand dollars."

"That's what we want, too," interrupted Mr. Berg with a smile.

"But," went on Tom's father, "since then certain matters have come up, and I think, on the whole, that we'll not compete for the prize after all."

"Not compete for the prize?" almost shouted the agent for Bentley & Eagert. "Why, the idea! You ought to compete. It is good for the trade. We think we have a very fine craft, and probably we would beat you in the tests, but——"

"I wouldn't be too sure of that," put in Tom. "You have only seen the outside of our boat. The inside is better yet."

"Ah, I have no doubt of that," spoke Mr. Berg, "but we have been at the business longer than you have, and have had more experience. Still we welcome competition. But I am very much surprised that you are not going to compete for the prize, Mr. Swift. Very much surprised, indeed! You see, I came down from Philadelphia to arrange so that we could both enter our ships at the same time. I understand there is another firm of submarine boat builders who are going to try for the prize, and I want to arrange a date that will be satisfactory to all. I am greatly astonished that you are not going to compete."

"Well, we were going to," said Mr. Swift, "only we have changed our minds, that's all. My son and I have other plans."

"May I ask what they are?" questioned Mr. Berg.

"You may," exclaimed Tom quickly; "but I don't believe we can tell you. They're a secret," he added more cordially.

"Oh, I see," retorted Mr. Berg. "Well, of course I don't wish to penetrate any of your secrets, but I hoped we could contest together for the Government prize. It is worth trying for, I assure you—fifty thousand dollars. Besides, there is the possibility of selling a number of submarines to the United States. It's a fine prize."

"But the one we are after is a bigger one," cried

Tom impetuously, and the moment he had spoken he wished he could recall the words.

"Eh? What's that?" exclaimed Mr. Berg. "You don't mean to say another government has offered a larger prize? If I had known that I would not have let my firm enter into the competition for the bonus offered by the United States. Please tell me——"

"I'm sorry," went on Tom more soberly. "I shouldn't have spoken. Mr. Berg, the plans of my father and myself are such that we can't reveal them now. We are going to try for a prize, but not in competition with you. It's an entirely different matter."

"Well, I guess you'll find that the firm of Bentley & Eagert are capable of trying for any prizes that are offered," boasted the agent. "We may be competitors yet."

"I don't believe so," replied Mr. Swift.

"We may," repeated Mr. Berg. "And if we do, please remember that we will show no mercy. Our boats are the best."

"And may the best boat win," interjected Mr. Sharp. "That's all we ask. A fair field and no favors."

"Of course," spoke the agent coldly. "Is this another son of yours?" he asked.

"No, but a good friend," replied the aged inventor. "No, Mr. Berg, we won't compete this time. You may tell your firm so."

"Very good," was the other's stiff reply. "Then I will bid you good night. We shall carry off the Government prize, but permit me to add that I am very much astonished, very much indeed, that you do not try for the prize. From what I have seen of your submarine you have a very good one, almost as good, in some respects, as ours. I bid you good night," and with a bow the man left the room and hurried away from the house.

CHAPTER IV

TOM IS IMPRISONED

"WELL, I must say he's a cool one," remarked Tom, as the echoes of Mr. Berg's steps died away. "The idea of thinking his boat better than ours! I don't like that man, dad. I'm suspicious of him. Do you think he came here to steal some of our ideas?"

"No, I hardly believe so, my son. But how did you discover him?"

"Just as you saw, dad. I heard a noise and went back there to investigate. I found him sneaking around, looking at the electric propeller plates. I went to grab him just as he stumbled over a board. At first I thought it was one of the old gang. I'm almost sure he was trying to discover something."

"No, Tom. The firm he works for are good business men, and they would not countenance anything like that. They are heartless competitors, however, and if they saw a legitimate chance to get ahead of me and take advantage, they would do it. But they would not sneak in to steal my ideas. I feel sure of that. Besides, they have a certain type of submarine which they think is the best ever invented, and they would hardly change at this late day. They feel sure of winning the Government prize, and I'm just as glad we're not going to have a contest."

"Do you think our boat is better than theirs?"

"Much better, in many respects."

"I don't like that man Berg, though," went on Tom.

"Nor do I," added his father. "There is something strange about him. He was very anxious that I should compete. Probably he thought his firm's boat would go so far ahead of ours that they would get an extra bonus. But I'm glad he didn't see our new method of propulsion. That is the principal improvement in the *Advance* over other types of submarines. Well, another week and we will be ready for the test."

"Have you known Mr. Berg long, dad?"

"Not very. I met him in Washington when I was in the patent office. He was taking out papers on a submarine for his firm at the same time I got mine for the *Advance*. It is rather curious that he should come all the way here from Philadelphia, merely to see if I was going to compete.

There is something strange about it, something that I can't understand."

The time was to come when Mr. Swift and his son were to get at the bottom of Mr. Berg's reasons, and they learned to their sorrow that he had penetrated some of their secrets.

Before going to bed that night Tom and Mr. Sharp paid a visit to the shed where the submarine was resting on the ways, ready for launching. They found Mr. Jackson on guard and the engineer said that no one had been around. Nor was anything found disturbed.

"It certainly is a great machine," remarked the lad as he looked up at the cigar-shaped bulk towering over his head. "Dad has outdone himself this trip."

"It looks all right," commented Mr. Sharp. "Whether it will work is another question."

"Yes, we can't tell until it's in the water," conceded Tom. "But I hope it does. Dad has spent much time and money on it."

The *Advance* was, as her name indicated, much in advance of previous submarines. There was not so much difference in outward construction as there was in the means of propulsion and in the manner in which the interior and the machinery were arranged.

The submarine planned by Mr. Swift and Tom

jointly, and constructed by them, with the aid of Mr. Sharp and Mr. Jackson, was shaped like a cigar, over one hundred feet long and twenty feet in diameter at the thickest part. It was divided into many compartments, all water-tight, so that if one or even three were flooded the ship would still be useable.

Buoyancy was provided for by having several tanks for the introduction of compressed air, and there was an emergency arrangement so that a collapsible aluminum container could be distended and filled with a powerful gas. This was to be used if, by any means, the ship was disabled on the bottom of the ocean. The container could be expanded and filled, and would send the *Advance* to the surface.

Another peculiar feature was that the engine-room, dynamos and other appartus were all contained amidships. This gave stability to the craft, and also enabled the same engine to operate both shafts and propellers, as well as both the negative forward electrical plates, and the positive rear ones.

These plates were a new idea in submarine construction, and were the outcome of an idea of Mr. Swift, with some suggestions from his son.

The aged inventor did not want to depend on the usual screw propellers for his craft, nor did

he want to use a jet of compressed air, shooting
out from a rear tube, nor yet a jet of water, by
means of which the creature called the squid
shoots himself along. Mr. Swift planned to send
the *Advance* along under water by means of electricity.

Certain peculiar plates were built at the forward and aft blunt noses of the submarine. Into
the forward plate a negative charge of electricity
was sent, and into the one at the rear a positive
charge, just as one end of a horseshoe magnet is
positive and will repel the north end of a compass needle, while the other pole of a magnet is
negative and will attract it. In electricity like
repels like, while negative and positive have a
mutual attraction for each other.

Mr. Swift figured out that if he could send a
powerful current of negative electricity into the
forward plate it would pull the boat along, for
water is a good conductor of electricity, while
if a positive charge was sent into the rear plate
it would serve to push the submarine along, and
he would thus get a pulling and pushing motion,
just as a forward and aft propeller works on
some ferry boats.

But the inventor did not depend on these plates
alone. There were auxiliary forward and aft
propellers of the regular type, so that if the

electrical plates did not work, or got out of order, the screws would serve to send the *Advance* along.

There was much machinery in the submarine. There were gasolene motors, since space was too cramped to allow the carrying of coal for boilers. There were dynamos, motors and powerful pumps. Some of these were for air, and some for water. To sink the submarine below the surface large tanks were filled with water. To insure a more sudden descent, deflecting rudders were also used, similar to those on an airship. There were also special air pumps, and one for the powerful gas, which was manufactured on board.

Forward from the engine-room was a cabin, where meals could be served, and where the travelers could remain in the daytime. There was also a small cooking galley, or kitchen, there. Back of the engine-room were the sleeping quarters and the storerooms. The submarine was steered from the forward compartment, and here were also levers, wheels and valves that controlled all the machinery, while a number of dials showed in which direction they were going, how deep they were, and at what speed they were moving, as well as what the ocean pressure was.

On top, forward, was a small conning, or observation tower, with auxiliary and steering and controlling apparatus there. This was to be used

when the ship was moving along on the surface
of the ocean, or merely with the deck awash.
There was a small flat deck surrounding the conning tower, and this was available when the craft
was on the surface.

There was provision made for leaving the ship
when it was on the bed of the ocean. When it
was desired to do this the occupants put on diving
suits, which were provided with portable oxygen
tanks. Then they entered a chamber into which
water was admitted until it was equal in pressure
to that outside. Then a steel door was opened,
and they could step out. To re-enter the ship
the operation was reversed. This was not a new
feature. In fact, many submarines to-day use it.

At certain places there were thick bull's-eye
windows, by means of which the under-water
travelers could look out into the ocean through
which they were moving. As a defense against
the attacks of submarine monsters there was a
steel, pointed ram, like a big harpoon. There
were also a bow and a stern electrical gun, of
which more will be told later.

In addition to ample sleeping accommodations
there were many conveniences aboard the
Advance. Plenty of fresh water could be carried,
and there was an apparatus for distilling more
from the sea water that surrounded the travelers.

Compressed air was carried in large tanks, and oxygen could be made as needed. In short, nothing that could add to the comfort or safety of the travelers had been omitted. There was a powerful crane and windlass, which had been installed when Mr. Swift thought his boat might be bought by the Government. This was to be used for raising wrecks or recovering objects from the bottom of the ocean. Ample stores and provisions were to be carried and, once the travelers were shut up in the *Advance,* they could exist for a month below the surface, providing no accident occurred.

All these things Tom and Mr. Sharp thought of as they looked over the ship before turning in for the night. The craft was made immensely strong to withstand powerful pressure at the bottom of the ocean. The submarine could penetrate to a depth of about three miles. Below that it was dangerous to go, as the awful force would crush the plates, powerful as they were.

"Well, we'll rush things to-morrow and the next day," observed Tom as he prepared to leave the building. "Then we'll soon see if it works."

For the next week there were busy times in the shop near the ocean. Great secrecy was maintained, and though curiosity seekers did stroll along now and then, they received little satisfaction. At first Mr. Swift thought that the visit of Mr. Berg would have unpleasant results, for he feared that the agent would talk about the craft, of which he had so unexpectedly gotten a sight. But nothing seemed to follow from his chance inspection, and it was forgotten.

It was one evening, about a week later, that Tom was alone in the shop. The two mechanics that had been hired to help out in the rush had been let go, and the ship needed but a few adjustments to make it ready for the sea.

"I think I'll just take another look at the water tank valves," said Tom to himself as he prepared to enter the big compartments which received the water ballast. "I want to be sure they work properly and quickly. We've got to depend on them to make us sink when we want to, and, what's more important, to rise to the surface in a hurry. I've got time enough to look them over before dad and Mr. Sharp get back."

Tom entered the starboard tank by means of an emergency sliding door between the big compartments and the main part of the ship. This was closed by a worm and screw gear, and once the ship was in the water would seldom be used.

The young inventor proceeded with his task, carefully inspecting the valves by the light of a lantern he carried. The apparatus seemed to be

all right, and Tom was about to leave when a
peculiar noise attracted his attention. It was
the sound of metal scraping on metal, and the
lad's quick and well-trained ear told him it was
somewhere about the ship.

He turned to leave the tank, but as he wheeled
around his light flashed on a solid wall of steel
back of him. The emergency outlet had been
closed! He was a prisoner in the water compartment, and he knew, from past experience, that
shout as he would, his voice could not be heard
ten feet away. His father and Mr. Sharp, as he
was aware, had gone to a near-by city for some
tools, and Mr. Jackson, the engineer, was temporarily away. Mrs. Baggert, in the house, could
not hear his cries.

"I'm locked in!" cried Tom aloud. "The worm
gear must have shut of itself. But I don't see
how that could be. I've got to get out mighty
soon, though, or I'll smother. This tank is airtight, and it won't take me long to breath up all
the oxygen there is here. I must get that slide
open."

He sought to grasp the steel plate that closed
the emergency opening. His fingers slipped over
the smooth, polished surface. He was hermetic-
ally sealed up—a captive! Blankly he set his

lantern down and leaned hopelessly against the wall of the tank.

"I've got to get out," he murmured.

As if in answer to him he heard a voice on the outside, crying:

"There, Tom Swift! I guess I've gotten even with you now! Maybe next time you won't take a reward away from me, and lick me into the bargain. I've got you shut up good and tight, and you'll stay there until I get ready to let you out."

"Andy Foger!" gasped Tom. "Andy Foger sneaked in here and turned the gear. But how did he get to this part of the coast? Andy Foger, you let me out!" shouted the young inventor; and as Andy's mocking laugh came to him faintly through the steel sides of the submarine, the imprisoned lad beat desperately with his hands on the smooth sides of the tank, vainly wondering how his enemy had discovered him.

CHAPTER V

Not for long did the young inventor endeavor to break his way out of the water-ballast tank by striking the heavy sides of it. Tom realized that this was worse than useless. He listened intently, but could hear nothing. Even the retreating footsteps of Andy Foger were inaudible.

"This certainly is a pickle!" exclaimed Tom aloud. "I can't understand how he ever got here. He must have traced us after we went to Shopton in the airship the last time. Then he sneaked in here. Probably he saw me enter, but how could he know enough to work the worm gear and close the door? Andy has had some experience with machinery, though, and one of the vaults in the bank where his father is a director closed just like this tank. That's very likely how he learned about it. But I've got to do something else besides thinking of that sneak, Andy. I've got to get out of here. Let's see if I can work the gear from inside."

40

Before he started, almost, Tom knew that it would be impossible. The tank was made to close from the interior of the submarine, and the heavy door, built to withstand the pressure of tons of water, could not be forced except by the proper means.

"No use trying that," concluded the lad, after a tiring attempt to force back the sliding door with his hands. "I've got to call for help."

He shouted until the vibrations in the confined space made his ears ring, and the mere exertion of raising his voice to the highest pitch made his heart beat quickly. Yet there came no response. He hardly expected that there would be any, for with his father and Mr. Sharp away, the engineer absent on an errand, and Mrs. Baggert in the house some distance off, there was no one to hear his calls for help, even if they had been capable of penetrating farther than the extent of the shed, where the under-water craft had been constructed.

"I've got to wait until some of them come out here," thought Tom. "They'll be sure to miss me and make a search. Then it will be easy enough to call to them and tell them where I am, once they are inside the shed. But——" He paused, for a horrible fear came over him. "Suppose they should come—too late?" The tank was airtight. There was enough air in it to last for some time, but, sooner or later, it would no longer support life. Already, Tom thought, it seemed oppressive, though probably that was his imagination.

"I must get out!" he repeated frantically. "I'll die in here—soon."

Again he tried to shove back the steel door. Then he repeated his cries until he was weary. No one answered him. He fancied once he could hear footsteps in the shed, and thought, perhaps, it was Andy, come back to gloat over him. Then Tom knew the red-haired coward would not dare venture back. We must do Andy the justice to say that he never realized that he was endangering Tom's life. The bully had no idea the tank was airtight when he closed it. He had seen Tom enter and a sudden whim came to him to revenge himself.

But that did not help the young inventor any. There was no doubt about it now—the air was becoming close. Tom had been imprisoned nearly two hours, and as he was a healthy, strong lad, he required plenty of oxygen. There was certainly less than there had been in the tank. His head began to buzz, and there was a ringing in his ears.

Once more he fell upon his knees, and his

fingers sought the small projections of the gear on the inside of the door. He could no more budge the mechanism than a child could open a burglar-proof vault.

"It's no use," he moaned, and he sprawled at full length on the floor of the tank, for there the air was purer. As he did so his fingers touched something. He started as they closed around the handle of a big monkey wrench. It was one he had brought into the place with him. Imbued with new hope he struck a match and lighted his lantern, which he had allowed to go out as it burned up too much of the oxygen. By the gleam of it he looked to see if there were any bolts or nuts he could loosen with the wrench, in order to slide the door back. It needed but a glance to show him the futility of this.

"It's no go," he murmured, and he let the wrench fall to the floor. There was a ringing, clanging sound, and as it smote his ears Tom sprang up with an exclamation.

"That's the thing!" he cried. "I wonder I didn't think of it before. I can signal for help by pounding on the sides of the tank with the wrench. The blows will carry a good deal farther than my voice would." Every one knows how far the noise of a boiler shop, with hammers falling on steel plates, can be heard; much farther than can a human voice.

Tom began a lusty tattoo on the metal sides of the tank. At first he merely rattled out blow after blow, and then, as another thought came to him, he adopted a certain plan. Some time previous, when he and Mr. Sharp had planned their trip in the air, the two had adopted a code of signals. As it was difficult in a high wind to shout from one end of the airship to the other, the young inventor would sometimes pound on a pipe which ran from the pilot house of the *Red Cloud* to the engine-room. By a combination of numbers, simple messages could be conveyed. The code included a call for help. Forty-seven was the number, but there had never been any occasion to use it.

Tom remembered this now. At once he ceased his indiscriminate hammering, and began to beat out regularly—one, two, three, four—then a pause, and seven blows would be given. Over and over again he rang out this number—forty-seven—the call for help.

"If Mr. Sharp only comes back he will hear that, even in the house," thought poor Tom. "Maybe Garret or Mrs. Baggert will hear it, too, but they won't know what it means. They'll think I'm just working on the submarine."

It seemed several hours to Tom that he pounded out that cry for aid, but, as he afterward learned, it was only a little over an hour. Signal after signal he sent vibrating from the steel sides of the tank. When one arm tired he would use the other. He grew weary, his head was aching, and there was a ringing in his ears; a ringing that seemed as if ten thousand bells were jangling out their peals, and he could barely distinguish his own pounding.

Signal after signal he sounded. It was becoming like a dream to him, when suddenly, as he paused for a rest, he heard his name called faintly, as if far away.

"Tom! Tom! Where are you?"

It was the voice of Mr. Sharp. Then followed the tones of the aged inventor.

"My poor boy! Tom, are you still alive?"

"Yes, dad! In the starboard tank!" the lad gasped out, and then he lost his senses. When he revived he was lying on a pile of bagging in the submarine shop, and his father and the aeronaut were bending over him.

"Are you all right, Tom?" asked Mr. Swift.

"Yes—I—I guess so," was the hesitating answer. "Yes," the lad added, as the fresh air cleared his head. "I'll be all right pretty soon. Have you seen Andy Foger?"

"Did he shut you in there?" demanded Mr. Swift.

Tom nodded.

"I'll have him arrested!" declared Mr. Swift. "I'll go to town as soon as you're in good shape again and notify the police."

"No, don't," pleaded Tom. "I'll take care of Andy myself. I don't really believe he knew how serious it was. I'll settle with him later, though."

"Well, it came mighty near being serious," remarked Mr. Sharp grimly. "Your father and I came back a little sooner than we expected, and as soon as I got near the house I heard your signal. I knew what it was in a moment. There were Mrs. Baggert and Garret talking away, and when I asked them why they didn't answer your call they said they thought you were merely tinkering with the machinery. But I knew better. It's the first time we ever had a use for 'forty-seven,' Tom."

"And I hope it will be the last," replied the young inventor with a faint smile. "But I'd like to know what Andy Foger is doing in this neighborhood."

Tom was soon himself again and able to go to the house, where he found Mrs. Baggert brewing a big basin of catnip tea, under the impression that it would in some way be good for him.

She could not forgive herself for not having answered his signal, and as for Mr. Jackson, he had started for a doctor as soon as he learned that Tom was shut up in the tank. The services of the medical man were canceled by telephone, as there was no need for him, and the engineer came back to the house.

Tom was fully himself the next day, and aided his father and Mr. Sharp in putting the finishing touches to the *Advance*. It was found that some alteration was required in the auxiliary propellers, and this, much to the regret of the young inventor, would necessitate postponing the trial a few days.

"But we'll have her in the water next Friday," promised Mr. Swift.

"Aren't you superstitious about Friday?" asked the balloonist.

"Not a bit of it," replied the aged inventor. "Tom," he added, "I wish you would go in the house and get me the roll of blueprints you'll find on my desk."

As the lad neared the cottage he saw, standing in front of the place, a small automobile. A man had just descended from it, and it needed but a glance to show that he was Mr. Addison Berg.

"Ah, good morning, Mr. Swift," greeted Mr.

Berg. "I wish to see your father, but as I don't wish to lay myself open to suspicions by entering the shop, perhaps you will ask him to step here."

"Certainly," answered the lad, wondering why the agent had returned. Getting the blueprints, and asking Mr. Berg to sit down on the porch, Tom delivered the message.

"You come back with me, Tom," said his father. "I want you to be a witness to what he says. I'm not going to get into trouble with these people."

Mr. Berg came to the point at once.

"Mr. Swift," he said, "I wish you would reconsider your determination not to enter the Government trials. I'd like to see you compete. So would my firm."

"There is no use going over that again," replied the aged inventor. "I have another object in view now than trying for the Government prize. What it is I can't say, but it may develop in time —if we are successful," and he looked at his son, smiling the while.

Mr. Berg tried to argue, but it was of no avail. Then he changed his manner, and said:

"Well, since you won't, you won't, I suppose. I'll go back and report to my firm. Have you

anything special to do this morning?" he went
on to Tom.

"Well, I can always find something to keep
me busy," replied the lad, "but as for anything
special——"

"I thought perhaps you'd like to go for a trip
in my auto," interrupted Mr. Berg. "I had asked
a young man who is stopping at the same hotel
where I am to accompany me, but he has unexpectedly left, and I don't like to go alone. His
name was—let me see. I have a wretched mem-
ory for names, but it was something like Roger
or Moger."

"Foger!" cried Tom. "Was it Andy Foger?"

"Yes, that was it. Why, do you know him?"
asked Mr. Berg in some surprise.

"I should say so," replied Tom. "He was the
cause of what might have resulted in something
serious for me," and the lad explained about being
imprisoned in the tank.

"You don't tell me!" cried Mr. Berg. "I had
no idea he was that kind of a lad. You see, his
father is one of the directors of the firm by whom
I am employed. Andy came from home to spend
a few weeks at the seaside, and stopped at the
same hotel that I did. He went off yesterday afternoon, and I haven't seen him since, though he
promised to go for a ride with me. He must have

come over here and entered your shop unobserved. I remember now he asked me where the submarine was being built that was going to compete with our firm's, and I told him. I didn't think he was that kind of a lad. Well, since he's probably gone back home, perhaps you will come for a ride with me, Tom."

"I'm afraid I can't go, thank you," answered the lad. "We are very busy getting our submarine in shape for a trial. But I can imagine why Andy left so hurriedly. He probably learned that a doctor had been summoned for me, though, as it happened, I didn't need one. But Andy probably got frightened at what he had done, and left. I'll make him more sorry, when I meet him."

"Don't blame you a bit," commented Mr. Berg. "Well, I must be getting back."

He hastened out to his auto, while Tom and his father watched the agent.

"Tom, never trust that man," advised the aged inventor solemnly.

"Just what I was about to remark," said his son. "Well, let's get back to work. Queer that he should come here again, and it's queer about Andy Foger."

Father and son returned to the machine shop, while Mr. Berg puffed away in his auto. A little later, Tom having occasion to go to a building near the boundary line of the cottage property which his father had hired for the season, saw, through the hedge that bordered it, an automobile standing in the road. A second glance showed him that it was Mr. Berg's machine. Something had gone wrong with it, and the agent had alighted to make an adjustment.

The young inventor was close to the man, though the latter was unaware of his presence.

"Hang it all!" Tom heard Mr. Berg exclaim to himself. "I wonder what they can be up to? They won't enter the Government contests, and they won't say why. I believe they're up to some game, and I've got to find out what it is. I wonder if I couldn't use this Foger chap?

"He seems to have it in for this Tom Swift," Mr. Berg went on, still talking to himself, though not so low but that Tom could hear him. "I think I'll try it. I'll get Andy Foger to sneak around and find out what the game is. He'll do it, I know."

By this time the auto was in working order again, and the agent took his seat and started off.

"So that's how matters lie, eh?" thought Tom. "Well, Mr. Berg, we'll be doubly on the lookout for you after this. As for Andy Foger, I think

I'll make him wish he'd never locked me in that tank. So you expect to find out our 'game,' eh, Mr. Berg? Well, when you do know it, I think it will astonish you. I only hope you don't learn what it is until we get at that sunken treasure, though."

But alas for Tom's hopes. Mr. Berg did learn of the object of the treasure-seekers, and sought to defeat them, as we shall learn as our story proceeds.

CHAPTER VI

TURNING THE TABLES

WHEN the young inventor informed his father what he had overheard Mr. Berg saying, the aged inventor was not as much worried as his son anticipated.

"All we'll have to do, Tom," he said, "is to keep quiet about where we are going. Once we have the *Advance* afloat, and try her out, we can start on our voyage for the South American coast and search for the sunken treasure. When we begin our voyage under water I defy any one to tell where we are going, or what our plans are. No, I don't believe we need worry about Mr. Berg, though he probably means mischief."

"Well, I'm going to keep my eyes open for him and Andy Foger," declared Tom.

The days that followed were filled with work. Not only were there many unexpected things to do about the submarine, but Mr. Sharp was kept busy making inquiries about the sunken treasure ship. These inquiries had to be made carefully, as the adventurers did not want their plans talked of, and nothing circulates more quickly than rumors of an expedition after treasure of any kind.

"What about the old sea captain you were going to get to go with us?" asked Mr. Swift of the balloonist one afternoon. "Have you succeeded in finding one yet?"

"Yes; I am in communication with a man I think will be just the person for us. His name is Captain Alden Weston, and he has sailed all over the world. He has also taken part in more than one revolution, and, in fact, is a soldier of fortune. I do not know him personally, but a friend of mine knows him, and says he will serve us faithfully. I have written to him, and he will be here in a few days."

"That's good. Now about the location of the wreck itself. Have you been able to learn any more details?"

"Well, not many. You see, the *Boldero* was abandoned in a storm, and the captain did not take very careful observations. As nearly as it can be figured out the treasure ship went to the bottom in latitude forty-five degrees south, and longitude twenty-seven east from Washington. That's a pretty indefinite location, but I hope,

once we get off the Uruguay coast, we can better
it. We can anchor or lay outside the harbor, and
in the small boat we carry go ashore and possibly gain more details. For it was at Montevideo that the shipwrecked passengers and sailors
landed."

"Does Captain Weston know our object?" inquired Tom.

"No, and I don't propose to tell him until we
are ready to start," replied Mr. Sharp. "I don't
know just how he'll consider a submarine trip
after treasure, but if I spring it on him suddenly
he's less likely to back out. Oh, I think he'll
go."

Somewhat unexpectedly the next day it was
discovered that certain tools and appliances were
needed for the submarine, and they had been left
in the house at Shopton, where Eradicate Sampson was in charge as caretaker during the absence
of Mr. Swift and his son and the housekeeper.

"Well, I suppose we'll have to go back after
them," remarked Tom. "We'll take the airship,
dad, and make a two-days' trip of it. Is there
anything else you want?"

"Well, you might bring a bundle of papers
you'll find in the lower right hand drawer of
my desk. They contain some memoranda I need."

Tom and Mr. Sharp had become so used to

traveling in the airship that it seemed no novelty to them, though they attracted much attention wherever they went. They soon had the *Red Cloud* in readiness for a flight, and rising in the air above the shop that contained the powerful submarine, a craft utterly different in type from the aeroplane, the nose of the airship was pointed toward Shopton.

They made a good flight and landed near the big shed where the bird of the air was kept. It was early evening when they got to the Swift homestead, and Eradicate Sampson was glad to see them.

Eradicate was a good cook, and soon had a meal ready for the travelers. Then, while Mr. Sharp selected the tools and other things needed, and put them in the airship ready for the start back the next morning, Tom concluded he would take a stroll into Shopton, to see if he could see his friend, Ned Newton. It was early evening, and the close of a beautiful day, a sharp shower in the morning having cooled the air.

Tom was greeted by a number of acquaintances ' as he strolled along, for, since the episode of the bank robbery, when he had so unexpectedly returned with the thieves and the cash, the lad was better known than ever.

"I guess Ned must be home," thought our hero

as he looked in vain for his chum among the
throng on the streets. "I've got time to take a
stroll down to his house."

Tom was about to cross the street when he
was startled by the sound of an automobile horn
loudly blown just at his side. Then a voice
called:

"Hey, there! Git out of the way if you don't
want to be run over!"

He looked up, and saw a car careening along.
At the wheel was the red-haired bully, Andy
Foger, and in the tonneau were Sam Snedecker
and Pete Bailey.

"Git out of the way," added Sam, and he
grinned maliciously at Tom.

The latter stepped back, well out of the path of
the car, which was not moving very fast. Just
in front of Tom was a puddle of muddy water.
There was no necessity for Andy steering into
it, but he saw his opportunity, and a moment later
one of the big pneumatic tires had plunged into
the dirty fluid, spattering it all over Tom, some
even going as high as his face.

"Ha! ha!" laughed Andy. "Maybe you'll get
out of my way next time, Tom Swift."

The young inventor was almost speechless from
righteous anger. He wiped the mud from his

face, glanced down at his clothes, which were all
but ruined, and called out:

"Hold on there, Andy Foger! I want to see
you!" for he thought of the time when Andy had
shut him in the tank.

"Ta! ta!" shouted Pete Bailey.

"See you later," added Sam.

"Better go home and take a bath, and then sail
away in your submarine," went on Andy. "I'll
bet it will sink."

Before Tom could reply the auto had turned
a corner. Disgusted and angry, he tried to sop
up some of the muddy water with his handker-
chief. While thus engaged he heard his name
called, and looked up to see Ned Newton.

"What's the matter? Fall down?" asked his
chum.

"Andy Foger," replied Tom.

"That's enough," retorted Ned. "I can guess
the rest. We'll have to tar and feather him some
day, and ride him out of town on a rail. I'd
lick him myself, only his father is a director in
the bank where I work, and I'd be fired if I did.
Can't afford any such pleasure. But some day
I'll give Andy a good trouncing, and then resign
before they can discharge me. But I'll be looking
for another job before I do that. Come on to
my house, Tom, and I'll help you clean up."

Tom was a little more presentable when he left his chum's residence, after spending the evening there, but he was still burning for revenge against Andy and his cronies. He had half a notion to go to Andy's house and tell Mr. Foger how nearly serious the bully's prank at the submarine had been, but he concluded that Mr. Foger would only uphold his son.

"No, I'll settle with him myself," decided Tom.

Bidding Eradicate keep a watchful eye about the house, and leaving word for Mr. Damon to be sure to come to the coast if he again called at the Shopton house, Tom and Mr. Sharp prepared to make their return trip early the next morning.

The gas tank was filled and the *Red Cloud* arose in the air. Then, with the propellers moving at moderate speed, the nose of the craft was pointed toward the New Jersey coast.

A few miles out from Shopton, finding there was a contrary wind in the upper regions where they were traveling, Mr. Sharp descended several hundred feet. They were moving over a sparsely settled part of the country, and looking down, Tom saw, speeding along a highway, an automobile.

"I wonder who's in it?" he remarked, taking down a telescope and peering over the window

ledge of the cabin. The next moment he uttered
a startled exclamation.

"Andy Foger, Sam Snedecker and Pete
Bailey!" he cried. "Oh, I wish I had a bucket
of water to empty on them."

"I know a better way to get even with them
than that," said Mr. Sharp.

"How?" asked Tom eagerly.

"I'll show you," replied the balloonist. "It's a
trick I once played on a fellow who did me an
injury. Here, you steer for a minute until I
get the thing fixed, then I'll take charge."

Mr. Sharp went to the storeroom and came
back with a long, stout rope and a small anchor
of four prongs. It was carried to be used in
emergencies, but so far had never been called into
requisition. Fastening the grapple to the cable,
the balloonist said:

"Now, Tom, they haven't seen you. You stand
in the stern and pay out the rope. I'll steer the
airship, and what I want you to do is to catch the
anchor in the rear of their car. Then I'll show
you some fun."

Tom followed instructions. Slowly he lowered
the rope with the dangling grapple. The airship
was also sent down, as the cable was not quite
long enough to reach the earth from the height
at which they were. The engine was run at

slow speed, so that the noise would not attract the attention of the three cronies who were speeding along, all unconscious of the craft in the air over their heads. The *Red Cloud* was moving in the same direction as was the automobile.

The anchor was now close to the rear of Andy's car. Suddenly it caught on the tonneau and Tom called that fact to Mr. Sharp.

"Fasten the rope at the cleat," directed the balloonist.

Tom did so, and a moment later the aeronaut sent the airship up by turning more gas into the container. At the same time he reversed the engine and the *Red Cloud* began pulling the touring car backward, also lifting the rear wheels clear from the earth.

A startled cry from the occupants of the machine told Tom and his friend that Andy and his cronies were aware something was wrong. A moment later Andy, looking up, saw the airship hovering in the air above him. Then he saw the rope fast to his auto. The airship was not rising now, or the auto would have been turned over, but it was slowly pulling it backward, in spite of the fact that the motor of the car was still going.

"Here! You let go of me!" cried Andy. "I'll have you arrested if you damage my car."

"Come up here and cut the rope," called Tom.

leaning over and looking down. He could enjoy the bully's discomfiture. As for Sam and Pete, they were much frightened, and cowered down on the floor of the tonneau.

"Maybe you'll shut me in the tank again and splash mud on me!" shouted Tom.

The rear wheels of the auto were lifted still higher from the ground, as Mr. Sharp turned on a little more gas. Andy was not proof against this.

"Oh! oh!" he cried. "Please let me down, Tom. I'm awful sorry for what I did! I'll never do it again! Please, please let me down! Don't! You'll tip me over!"

He had shut off his motor now, and was frantically clinging to the steering wheel.

"Do you admit that you're a sneak and a coward?" asked Tom, "rubbing it in."

"Yes, yes! Oh, please let me down!"

"Shall we?" asked Tom of Mr. Sharp.

"Yes," replied the balloonist. "We can afford to lose the rope and anchor for the sake of turning the tables. Cut the cable."

Tom saw what was intended. Using a little hatchet, he severed the rope with a single blow. With a crash that could be heard up in the air where the *Red Cloud* hovered, the rear wheels of the auto dropped to the ground. Then came two loud reports.

"Both tires busted!" commented Mr. Sharp dryly, and Tom, looking down, saw the trio of lads ruefully contemplating the collapsed rubber of the rear wheels. The tables had been effectually turned on Andy Foger. His auto was disabled, and the airship, with a graceful sweep, mounted higher and higher, continuing on its way to the coast.

CHAPTER VII

"WELL, I guess they've had their lesson," remarked Tom, as he took an observation through the telescope and saw Andy and his cronies hard at work trying to repair the ruptured tires. "That certainly was a corking good trick."

"Yes," admitted Mr. Sharp modestly. "I once did something similar, only it was a horse and wagon instead of an auto. But let's try for another speed record. The conditions are just right."

They arrived at the coast much sooner than they had dared to hope, the *Red Cloud* proving herself a veritable wonder.

The remainder of that day, and part of the next, was spent in working on the submarine.

"We'll launch her day after to-morrow," declared Mr. Swift enthusiastically. "Then to see whether my calculations are right or wrong."

64

"It won't be your fault if it doesn't work," said his son. "You certainly have done your best."

"And so have you and Mr. Sharp and the others, for that matter. Well, I have no doubt but that everything will be all right, Tom."

"There!" exclaimed Mr. Sharp the next morning, as he was adjusting a certain gage. "I knew I'd forget something. That special brand of lubricating oil. I meant to bring it from Shopton, and I didn't."

"Maybe I can get it in Atlantis," suggested Tom, naming the coast city nearest to them. "I'll take a walk over. It isn't far."

"Will you? I'll be glad to have you," resumed the balloonist. "A gallon will be all we'll need."

Tom was soon on his way. He had to walk, as the roads were too poor to permit him to use the motor-cycle, and the airship attracted too much attention to use on a short trip. He was strolling along, when from the other side of a row of sand dunes, that lined the uncertain road to Atlantis, he heard some one speaking. At first the tones were not distinct, but as the lad drew nearer to the voice he heard an exclamation.

"Bless my gold-headed cane! I believe I'm lost. He said it was out this way somewhere, but I don't see anything of it. If I had that Eradi-

cate Sampson here now I'd—bless my shoelaces!
I don't know what I would do to him."

"Mr. Damon! Mr. Damon!" cried Tom. "Is
that you?"

"Me? Of course it's me! Who else would it
be?" answered the voice. "But who are you?
Why, bless my liver! If it isn't Tom Swift!" he
cried. "Oh, but I'm glad to see you! I was
afraid I was shipwrecked! Bless my gaiters, how
are you, anyhow? How is your father? How is
Mr. Sharp, and all the rest of them?"

"Pretty well. And you?"

"Me? Oh, I'm all right; only a trifle nervous.
I called at your house in Shopton yesterday, and
Eradicate told me, as well as he could, where you
were located. I had nothing to do, so I thought
I'd take a run down here. But what's this I
hear about you? Are you going on a voyage?"

"Yes."

"In the air? May I go along again? I cer-
tainly enjoyed my other trip in the *Red Cloud*.
That is, all but the fire and being shot at. May
I go?"

"We're going on a different sort of trip this
time," said the youth.

"Where?"

"Under water."

"Under water? Bless my sponge bath! You don't mean it!"

"Yes. Dad has completed the submarine he was working on when we were off in the airship, and it will be launched the day after to-morrow."

"Oh, that's so. I'd forgotten about it. He's going to try for the Government prize, isn't he? But tell me more about it. Bless my scarf-pin, but I'm glad I met you! Going into town, I take it. Well, I just came from there, but I'll walk back with you. Do you think—is there any possibility —that I could go with you? Of course, I don't want to crowd you, but——"

"Oh, there'll be plenty of room," replied the young inventor. "In fact, more. room than we had in the airship. We were talking only the other day about the possibility of you going with us, but we didn't think you'd risk it."

"Risk it? Bless my liver! Of course I'll risk it! It can't be as bad as sailing in the air. You can't fall, that's certain."

"No; but maybe you can't rise," remarked Tom grimly.

"Oh, we won't think of that. Of course, I'd like to go. I fully expected to be killed in the *Red Cloud,* but as I wasn't I'm ready to take a chance in the water. On the whole, I think I prefer to be buried at sea, anyhow. Now, then, will you take me?"

"I think I can safely promise," answered Tom with a smile at his friend's enthusiasm.

The two were approaching the city, having walked along as they talked. There were still some sand dunes near the road, and they kept on the side of these, nearest the beach, where they could watch the breakers.

"But you haven't told me where you are going," went on Mr. Damon, after blessing a few dozen objects. "Where do the Government trials take place?"

"Well," replied the lad, "to be frank with you, we have abandoned our intention of trying for the Government prize."

"Not going to try for it? Bless my slippers! Why not? Isn't fifty thousand dollars worth striving for? And, with the kind of a submarine you say you have, you ought to be able to win."

"Yes, probably we could win," admitted the young inventor, "but we are going to try for a better prize."

"A better one? I don't understand."

"Sunken treasure," explained Tom. "There's a ship sunk off the coast of Uruguay, with three hundred thousand dollars in gold bullion aboard. Dad and I are going to try to recover that in our submarine. We're going to start day after to-morrow, and, if you like, you may go along."

"Go along! Of course I'll go along!" cried the eccentric man. "But I never heard of such a thing. Sunken treasure! Three hundred thousand dollars in gold! My, what a lot of money! And to go after it in a submarine! It's as good as a story!"

"Yes, we hope to recover all the treasure," said the lad. "We ought to be able to claim at least half of it."

"Bless my pocketbook!" cried Mr. Damon, but Tom did not hear him. At that instant his attention was attracted by seeing two men emerge from behind the sand dune near which he and Mr. Damon had halted momentarily, when the youth explained about the treasure. The man looked sharply at Tom. A moment later the first man was joined by another, and at the sight of him our hero could not repress an exclamation of alarm. For the second man was none other than Addison Berg.

The latter glanced quickly at Tom, and then, with a hasty word to his companion, the two swung around and made off in the opposite direction to that in which they had been walking.

"What's the matter?" asked Mr. Damon, see-ing the young inventor was strangely affected.

"That—that man," stammered the lad.

"You don't mean to tell me that was one of the Happy Harry gang, do you?"

"No. But one, or both of those men, may prove to be worse. That second man was Addison Berg, and he's agent for a firm of submarine boat builders who are rivals of dad's. Berg has been trying to find out why we abandoned our intention of competing for the Government prize."

"I hope you didn't tell him."

"I didn't intend to," replied Tom, smiling grimly, "but I'm afraid I have, however. He certainly overheard what I said. I spoke too loud. Yes, he must have heard me. That's why he hurried off so."

"Possibly no harm is done. You didn't give the location of the sunken ship."

"No; but I guess from what I said it will be easy enough to find. Well, if we're going to have a fight for the possession of that sunken gold, I'm ready for it. The *Advance* is well equipped for a battle. I must tell dad of this. It's my fault."

"And partly mine, for asking you such leading questions in a public place," declared Mr. Damon. "Bless my coat-tails, but I'm sorry! Maybe, after all, those men were so interested in what they

themselves were saying that they didn't understand what you said."

But if there had been any doubts on this score
they would have been dissolved had Tom and
his friend been able to see the actions of Mr.
Berg and his companion a little later. The plans
of the treasure-hunters had been revealed to their
enemies.

CHAPTER VIII

ANOTHER TREASURE EXPEDITION

WHILE Tom and Mr. Damon continued on to Atlantis after the oil, the young inventor lamenting from time to time that his remarks about the real destination of the *Advance* had been overheard by Mr. Berg, the latter and his companion were hastening back along the path that ran on one side of the sand dunes.

"What's your hurry?" asked Mr. Maxwell, who was with the submarine agent. "You turned around as if you were shot when you saw that man and the lad. There didn't appear to be any cause for such a hurry. From what I could hear they were talking about a submarine. You're in the same business. You might be friends."

"Yes, we might," admitted Mr. Berg with a peculiar smile; "but, unless I'm very much mistaken, we're going to be rivals."

"Rivals? What do you mean?"

"I can't tell you now. Perhaps I may later.

But if you don't mind, walk a little faster, please. I want to get to a long-distance telephone."

"What for?"

"I have just overheard something that I wish to communicate to my employers, Bentley & Eagert."

"Overheard something? I don't see what it could be, unless that lad——"

"You'll learn in good time," went on the submarine agent. "But I must telephone at once."

A little later the two men had reached a trolley line that ran into Atlantis, and they arrived at the city before Mr. Damon and Tom got there, as the latter had to go by a circuitous route. Mr. Berg lost no time in calling up his firm by telephone.

"I have had another talk with Mr. Swift," he reported to Mr. Bentley, who came to the instrument in Philadelphia.

"Well, what does he say?" was the impatient question. "I can't understand his not wanting to try for the Government prize. It is astonishing. You said you were going to discover the reason, Mr. Berg, but you haven't done so."

"I have."

"What is it?"

"Well, the reason Mr. Swift and his son don't care to try for the fifty thousand dollar prize is that they are after one of three hundred thousand dollars."

"Three hundred thousand dollars!" cried Mr. Bentley. "What government is going to offer such a prize as that for submarines, when they are getting almost as common as airships? We ought to have a try for that ourselves. What government is it?"

"No government at all. But I think we ought to have a try for it, Mr. Bentley."

"Explain."

"Well, I have just learned, most accidentally, that the Swifts are going after sunken treasure—three hundred thousand dollars in gold bullion."

"Sunken treasure? Where?"

"I don't know exactly, but off the coast of Uruguay," and Mr. Berg rapidly related what he had overheard Tom tell Mr. Damon. Mr. Bentley was much excited and impatient for more details, but his agent could not give them to him.

"Well," concluded the senior member of the firm of submarine boat builders, "if the Swifts are going after treasure, so can we. Come to Philadelphia at once, Mr. Berg, and we'll talk this matter over. There is no time to lose. We can afford to forego the Government prize for the chance of getting a much larger one. We have as much right to search for the sunken gold

as the Swifts have. Come here at once, and we
will make our plans."

"All right," agreed the agent with a smile as he
hung up the receiver. "I guess," he murmured
to himself, "that you won't be so high and mighty
with me after this, Tom Swift. We'll see who
has the best boat, after all. We'll have a contest
and a competition, but not for a government
prize. It will be for the sunken gold."

It was easy to see that Mr. Berg was much
pleased with himself.

Meanwhile, Tom and Mr. Damon had reached
Atlantis, and had purchased the oil. They started
back, but Tom took a street leading toward the
center of the place, instead of striking for the
beach path, along which they had come.

"Where are you going?" asked Mr. Damon.

"I want to see if that Andy Foger has come
back here," replied the lad, and he told of having
been shut in the tank by the bully.

"I've never properly punished him for that
trick," he went on, "though we did manage to
burst his auto tires. I'm curious to know how he
knew enough to turn that gear and shut the tank
door. He must have been loitering near the shop,
seen me go in the submarine alone, watched his
chance and sneaked in after me. But I'd like to
get a complete explanation, and if I once got hold

of Andy I could make him talk," and Tom clenched his fist in a manner that augured no good for the squint-eyed lad. "He was stopping at the same hotel with Mr. Berg, and he hurried away after the trick he played on me. I next saw him in Shopton, but I thought perhaps he might have come back here. I'm going to inquire at the hotel," he added.

Andy's name was not on the register since his hasty flight, however, and Tom, after inquiring from the clerk and learning that Mr. Berg was still a guest at the hostelry, rejoined Mr. Damon.

"Bless my hat!" exclaimed that eccentric individual as they started back to the lonely beach where the submarine was awaiting her advent into the water. "The more I think of the trip I'm going to take, the more I like it."

"I hope you will," remarked Tom. "It will be a new experience for all of us. There's only one thing worrying me, and that is about Mr. Berg having overheard what I said."

"Oh, don't worry about that. Can't we slip away and leave no trace in the water?"

"I hope so, but I must tell dad and Mr. Sharp about what happened."

The aged inventor was not a little alarmed at what his son related, but he agreed with Mr. Damon, whom he heartily welcomed, that little was to be apprehended from Berg and his employers.

"They know we're after a sunken wreck, but that's all they do know," said Tom's father. "We are only waiting for the arrival of Captain Alden Weston, and then we will go. Even if Bentley & Eagert make a try for the treasure we'll have the start of them, and this will be a case of first come, first served. Don't worry, Tom. I'm glad you're going, Mr. Damon. Come, I will show you our submarine."

As father and son, with their guest, were going to the machine shop, Mr. Sharp met them. He had a letter in his hand.

"Good news!" the balloonist cried. "Captain Weston will be with us to-morrow. He will arrive at the Beach Hotel in Atlantis, and wants one of us to meet him there. He has considerable information about the wreck."

"The Beach Hotel," murmured Tom. "That is where Mr. Berg is stopping. I hope he doesn't worm any of our secret from Captain Weston," and it was with a feeling of uneasiness that the young inventor continued after his father and Mr. Damon to where the submarine was.

CHAPTER IX

CAPTAIN WESTON'S ADVENT

"Bless my water ballast, but that certainly is a fine boat!" cried Mr. Damon, when he had been shown over the new craft. "I think I shall feel even safer in that than in the *Red Cloud.*"

"Oh, don't go back on the airship!" exclaimed Mr. Sharp. "I was counting on taking you on another trip."

"Well, maybe after we get back from under the ocean," agreed Mr. Damon. "I particularly like the cabin arrangements of the *Advance.* I think I shall enjoy myself."

He would be hard to please who could not take pleasure from a trip in the submarine. The cabin was particularly fine, and the sleeping arrangements were good.

More supplies could be carried than was possible on the airship, and there was more room in which to cook and serve food. Mr. Damon was fond of good living, and the kitchen pleased him as much as anything else.

78

Early the next morning Tom set out for Atlantis, to meet Captain Weston at the hotel. The
young inventor inquired of the clerk whether the
seafaring man had arrived, and was told that
he had come the previous evening.

"Is he in his room?" asked Tom.

"No," answered the clerk with a peculiar grin.
"He's an odd character. Wouldn't go to bed
last night until we had every window in his
room open, though it was blowing quite hard,
and likely to storm. The captain said he was
used to plenty of fresh air. Well, I guess he got
it, all right."

"Where is he now?" asked the youth, wondering what sort of an individual he was to meet.

"Oh, he was up before sunrise, so some of the
scrubwomen told me. They met him coming
from his room, and he went right down to the
beach with a big telescope he always carries with
him. He hasn't come back yet. Probably he's
down on the sand."

"Hasn't he had breakfast?"

"No. He left word he didn't want to eat until
about four bells, whatever time that is."

"It's ten o'clock," replied Tom, who had been
studying up on sea terms lately. "Eight bells is
eight o'clock in the morning, or four in the afternoon or eight at night, according to the time of

day. Then there's one bell for every half hour, so four bells this morning would be ten o'clock in this watch, I suppose."

"Oh, that's the way it goes, eh?" asked the clerk. "I never could get it through my head. What is twelve o'clock noon?"

"That's eight bells, too; so is twelve o'clock midnight. Eight bells is as high as they go on a ship. But I guess I'll go down and see if I can meet the captain. It will soon be ten o'clock, or four bells, and he must be hungry for breakfast. By the way, is that Mr. Berg still here?"

"No; he went away early this morning. He and Captain Weston seemed to strike up quite an acquaintance, the night clerk told me. They sat and smoked together until long after midnight, or eight bells," and the clerk smiled as he glanced down at the big diamond ring on his little finger.

"They did?" fairly exploded Tom, for he had visions of what the wily Mr. Berg might worm out of the simple captain.

"Yes. Why, isn't the captain a proper man to make friends with?" and the clerk looked at Tom curiously.

"Oh, yes, of course," was the hasty answer. "I guess I'll go and see if I can find him—the captain, I mean."

Tom hardly knew what to think. He wished his father, or Mr. Sharp, had thought to warn Captain Weston against talking of the wreck. It might be too late now.

The young inventor hurried to the beach, which was not far from the hotel. He saw a solitary figure pacing up and down, and from the fact that the man stopped, every now and then, and gazed seaward through a large telescope, the lad concluded it was the captain for whom he was in search. He approached, his footsteps making no sound on the sand. The man was still gazing through the glass.

"Captain Weston?" spoke Tom.

Without a show of haste, though the voice must have startled him, the captain turned. Slowly he lowered the telescope, and then he replied softly:

"That's my name. Who are you, if I may ask?"

Tom was struck, more than by anything else, by the gentle voice of the seaman. He had prepared himself, from the description of Mr. Sharp, to meet a gruff, bewhiskered individual, with a voice like a crosscut saw, and a rolling gait. Instead he saw a man of medium size, with a smooth face, merry blue eyes, and the softest voice and gentlest manner imaginable. Tom was very much disappointed. He had looked for a regular sea-dog, and he met a landsman, as he said afterward. But it was not long before our hero changed his mind regarding Captain Weston.

"I'm Tom Swift," the owner of that name said, "and I have been sent to show you the way to where our ship is ready to launch." The young inventor refrained from mentioning submarine, as it was the wish of Mr. Sharp to disclose this feature of the voyage to the sailor himself.

"Ha, I thought as much," resumed the captain quietly. "It's a fine day, if I may be permitted to say so," and he seemed to hesitate, as if there was some doubt whether or not he might make that observation.

"It certainly is," agreed the lad. Then, with a smile he added: "It is nearly eight bells."

"Ha!" exclaimed the captain, also smiling, but even his manner of saying "Ha!" was less demonstrative than that of most persons. "I believe I am getting hungry, if I may be allowed the remark," and again he seemed asking Tom's pardon for mentioning the fact.

"Perhaps you will come back to the cabin and have a little breakfast with me," he went on. "I don't know what sort of a galley or cook they have aboard the Beach Hotel, but it can't be much worse than some I've tackled."

"No, thank you," answered the youth. "I've had my breakfast. But I'll wait for you, and then I'd like to get back. Dad and Mr. Sharp are anxious to meet you."

"And I am anxious to meet them, if you don't mind me mentioning it," was the reply, as the captain once more put the spyglass to his eye and took an observation. "Not many sails in sight this morning," he added. "But the weather is fine, and we ought to get off in good shape to hunt for the treasure about which Mr. Sharp wrote me. I believe we are going after treasure," he said; "that is, if you don't mind talking about it."

"Not in the least," replied Tom quickly, thinking this a good opportunity for broaching a subject that was worrying him. "Did you meet a Mr. Berg here last night, Captain Weston?" he went on.

"Yes. Mr. Berg and I had quite a talk. He is a well-informed man."

"Did he mention the sunken treasure?" asked the lad, eager to find out if his suspicions were true.

"Yes, he did, if you'll excuse me putting it so plainly," answered the seaman, as if Tom might be offended at so direct a reply. But the young inventor was soon to learn that this was only an odd habit with the seaman.

"Did he want to know where the wreck of the *Boldero* was located?" continued the lad. "That is, did he try to discover if you knew anything about it?"

"Yes," said Mr. Weston, "he did. He pumped me, if you are acquainted with that term, and are not offended by it. You see, when I arrived here I made inquiries as to where your father's place was located. Mr. Berg overheard me, and introduced himself as agent for a shipbuilding concern. He was very friendly, and when he said he knew you and your parent, I thought he was all right."

Tom's heart sank. His worst fears were to be realized, he thought.

"Yes, he and I talked considerable, if I may be permitted to say so," went on the captain. "He seemed to know about the wreck of the *Boldero,* and that she had three hundred thousand dollars in gold aboard. The only thing he didn't know was where the wreck was located. He knew it was off Uruguay somewhere, but just where he couldn't say. So he asked me if I knew, since he must have concluded that I was going with you on the gold-hunting expedition."

"And you do know, don't you?" asked Tom eagerly.

"Well, I have it pretty accurately charted out, if you will allow me that expression," was the calm answer. "I took pains to look it up at the request of Mr. Sharp."

"And he wanted to worm that information out of you?" inquired the youth excitedly.

"Yes, I'm afraid he did."

"Did you give him the location?"

"Well," remarked the captain, as he took another observation before closing up the telescope, "you see, while we were talking, I happened to drop a copy of a map I'd made, showing the location of the wreck. Mr. Berg picked it up to hand to me, and he looked at it."

"Oh!" cried Tom. "Then he knows just where the treasure is, and he may get to it ahead of us. It's too bad."

"Yes," continued the seaman calmly, "Mr. Berg picked up that map, and he looked very closely at the latitude and longitude I had marked as the location of the wreck."

"Then he won't have any trouble finding it," murmured our hero.

"Eh? What's that?" asked the captain, "if I may be permitted to request you to repeat what you said."

"I say he won't have any trouble locating the sunken *Boldero*," repeated Tom.

"Oh, but I think he will, if he depends on that map," was the unexpected reply. "You see," explained Mr. Weston, "I'm not so simple as I look. I sensed what Mr. Berg was after, the minute he began to talk to me. So I fixed up a little game on him. The map which I dropped on purpose, not accidentally, where he would see it, did have the location of the wreck marked. Only it didn't happen to be the right location. It was about five hundred miles out of the way, and I rather guess if Mr. Berg and his friends go there for treasure they'll find considerable depth of water and quite a lonesome spot. Oh, no, I'm not as easy as I look, if you don't mind me mentioning that fact; and when a scoundrel sets out to get the best of me, I generally try to turn the tables on him. I've seen such men as Mr. Berg before. I'm afraid, I'm very much afraid, the sight he had of the fake map I made won't do him much good. Well, I declare, it's past four bells. Let's go to breakfast, if you don't mind me asking you," and with that the captain started off up the beach, Tom following, his ideas all in a whirl at the unlooked-for outcome of the interview.

CHAPTER X

Tom felt such a relief at hearing of Captain Weston's ruse that his appetite, sharpened by an early breakfast and the sea air, came to him with a rush, and he had a second morning meal with the odd sea captain, who chuckled heartily when he thought of how Mr. Berg had been deceived.

"Yes," resumed Captain Weston, over his bacon and eggs, "I sized him up for a slick article as soon as I laid eyes on him. But he evidently misjudged me, if I may be permitted that term. Oh, well, we may meet again, after we secure the treasure, and then I can show him the real map of the location of the wreck."

"Then you have it?" inquired the lad eagerly.

Captain Weston nodded, before hiding his face behind a large cup of coffee; his third, by the way.

"Let me see it?" asked Tom quickly.

The captain set down his cup. He looked care-

87

fully about the hotel dining-room. There were several guests, who, like himself, were having a late breakfast.

"It's a good plan," the sailor said slowly, "when you're going into unknown waters, and don't want to leave a wake for the other fellow to follow, to keep your charts locked up. If it's all the same to you," he added diffidently, "I'd rather wait until we get to where your father and Mr. Sharp are before displaying the real map. I've no objection to showing you the one Mr. Berg saw," and again he chuckled.

The young inventor blushed at his indiscretion. He felt that the news of the search for the treasure had leaked out through him, though he was the one to get on the trail of it by seeing the article in the paper. Now he had nearly been guilty of another break. He realized that he must be more cautious. The captain saw his confusion, and said:

"I know how it is. You're eager to get under way. I don't blame you. I was the same myself when I was your age. But we'll soon be at your place, and then I'll tell you all I know. Sufficient, now, to say that I believe I have located the wreck within a few miles. I got on the track of a sailor who had met one of the shipwrecked crew of the *Boldero,* and he gave me valuable information. Now tell me about the craft we are going in. A good deal depends on that."

Tom hardly knew what to answer. He recalled what Mr. Sharp had said about not wanting to tell Captain Weston, until the last moment, that they were going in a submarine, for fear the old seaman (for he was old in point of service though not in years) might not care to risk an under-water trip. Therefore Tom hesitated. Seeing it, Captain Weston remarked quietly:

"I mean, what type is your submarine? Does it go by compressed air, or water power?"

"How do you know it's a submarine?" asked the young inventor quickly, and in some confusion.

"Easy enough. When Mr. Berg thought he was pumping me, I was getting a lot of information from him. He told me about the submarine his firm was building, and, naturally, he mentioned yours. One thing led to another until I got a pretty good idea of your craft. What do you call it?"

"The *Advance.*"

"Good name. I like it, if you don't mind me speaking of it."

"We were afraid you wouldn't like it," commented Tom.

"What, the name?"

"No, the idea of going in a submarine."

"Oh," and Captain Weston laughed. "Well, it takes more than that to frighten me, if you'll excuse the expression. I've always had a hankering to go under the surface, after so many years spent on top. Once or twice I came near going under, whether I wanted to or not, in wrecks, but I think I prefer your way. Now, if you're all done, and don't mind me speaking of it, I think we'll start for your place. We must hustle, for Berg may yet get on our trail, even if he has got the wrong route," and he laughed again.

It was no small relief to Mr. Swift and Mr. Sharp to learn that Captain Weston had no objections to a submarine, as they feared he might have. The captain, in his diffident manner, made friends at once with the treasure-hunters, and he and Mr. Damon struck up quite an acquaintance. Tom told of his meeting with the seaman, and the latter related, with much gusto, the story of how he had fooled Mr. Berg.

"Well, perhaps you'd like to come and take a look at the craft that is to be our home while we're beneath the water," suggested Mr. Swift and the sailor assenting, the aged inventor, with much pride, assisted by Tom, pointed out on the *Advance* the features of interest. Captain Weston gave hearty approval, making one or two minor suggestions, which were carried out.

"And so you launch her to-morrow," he concluded, when he had completed the inspection. "Well, I hope it's a success, if I may be permitted to say so."

There were busy times around the machine shop next day. So much secrecy had been maintained that none of the residents, or visitors to the coast resort, were aware that in their midst was such a wonderful craft as the submarine. The last touches were put on the under-water ship; the ways, leading from the shop to the creek, were well greased, and all was in readiness for the launching. The tide would soon be at flood, and then the boat would slide down the timbers (at least, that was the hope of all), and would float in the element meant to receive her. It was decided that no one should be aboard when the launching took place, as there was an element of risk attached, since it was not known just how buoyant the craft was. It was expected she would float, until the filled tanks took her to the bottom, but there was no telling.

"It will be flood tide now in ten minutes," remarked Captain Weston quietly, looking at his watch. Then he took an observation through the telescope. "No hostile ships hanging in the offing," he reported. "All is favorable, if you don't mind me saying so," and he seemed afraid lest his remark might give offense.

"Get ready," ordered Mr. Swift. "Tom, see that the ropes are all clear," for it had been decided to ease the *Advance* down into the water by means of strong cables and windlasses, as the creek was so narrow that the submarine, if launched in the usual way, would poke her nose into the opposite mud bank and stick there.

"All clear," reported the young inventor.

"High tide!" exclaimed the captain a moment later, snapping shut his watch.

"Let go!" ordered Mr. Swift, and the various windlasses manned by the inventor, Tom and the others began to unwind their ropes. Slowly the ship slid along the greased ways. Slowly she approached the water. How anxiously they all watched her! Nearer and nearer her blunt nose, with the electric propulsion plate and the auxiliary propeller, came to the creek, the waters of which were quiet now, awaiting the turn of the tide.

Now little waves lapped the steel sides. It was the first contact of the *Advance* with her native element.

"Pay out the rope faster!" cried Mr. Swift.

The windlasses were turned more quickly. Foot by foot the craft slid along until, with a final rush, the stern left the ways and the submarine was afloat. Now would come the test. Would she ride on an even keel, or sink out of sight, or turn turtle? They all ran to the water's edge, Tom in the lead.

"Hurrah!" suddenly yelled the lad, trying to stand on his head. "She floats! She's a success! Come on! Let's get aboard!"

For, true enough, the *Advance* was riding like a duck on the water. She had been proportioned just right, and her lines were perfect. She rode as majestically as did any ship destined to sail on the surface, and not intended to do double duty.

"Come on, we must moor her to the pier," directed Mr. Sharp. "The tide will turn in a few minutes and take her out to sea."

He and Tom entered a small boat, and soon the submarine was tied to a small dock that had been built for the purpose.

"Now to try the engine," suggested Mr. Swift, who was almost trembling with eagerness; for the completion of the ship meant much to him.

"One moment," begged Captain Weston. "If you don't mind, I'll take an observation," he went on, and he swept the horizon with his telescope. "All clear," he reported. "I think we may go aboard and make a trial trip."

Little time was lost in entering the cabin and engine-room, Garret Jackson accompanying the party to aid with the machinery. It did not take long to start the motors, dynamos and the big gasolene engine that was the vital part of the craft. A little water was admitted to the tanks for ballast, since the food and other supplies were not yet on board. The *Advance* now floated with the deck aft of the conning tower showing about two feet above the surface of the creek. Mr. Swift and Tom entered the pilot house.

"Start the engines," ordered the aged inventor, "and we'll try my new system of positive and negative electrical propulsion."

There was a hum and whirr in the body of the ship beneath the feet of Tom and his father. Captain Weston stood on the little deck near the conning tower.

"All ready?" asked the youth through the speaking tube to Mr. Sharp and Mr. Jackson in the engine-room.

"All ready," came the answer.

Tom threw over the connecting lever, while his father grasped the steering wheel. The *Advance* shot forward, moving swiftly along, about half submerged.

"She goes! She goes!" cried Tom.

"She certainly does, if I may be permitted to

say so," was the calm contribution of Captain Weston. "I congratulate you."

Faster and faster went the new craft. Mr. Swift headed her toward the open sea, but stopped just before passing out of the creek, as he was not yet ready to venture into deep water.

"I want to test the auxiliary propellers," he said. After a little longer trial of the electric propulsion plates, which were found to work satisfactorily, sending the submarine up and down the creek at a fast rate, the screws, such as are used on most submarines, were put into gear. They did well, but were not equal to the plates, nor was so much expected of them.

"I am perfectly satisfied," announced Mr. Swift as he once more headed the boat to sea. "I think, Captain Weston, you had better go below now."

"Why so?"

"Because I am going to completely submerge the craft. Tom, close the conning tower door. Perhaps you will come in here with us, Captain Weston, though it will be rather a tight fit."

"Thank you, I will. I want to see how it feels to be in a pilot house under water."

Tom closed the water-tight door of the conning tower. Word was sent through the tube to the engine-room that a more severe test of the ship was about to be made. The craft was now outside the line of breakers and in the open sea.

"Is everything ready, Tom?" asked his father in a quiet voice.

"Everything," replied the lad nervously, for the anticipation of being about to sink below the surface was telling on them all, even on the calm, old sea captain.

"Then open the tanks and admit the water," ordered Mr. Swift.

His son turned a valve and adjusted some levers. There was a hissing sound, and the *Advance* began sinking. She was about to dive beneath the surface of the ocean, and those aboard her were destined to go through a terrible experience before she rose again.

CHAPTER XI

ON THE OCEAN BED

LOWER and lower sank the submarine. There was a swirling and foaming of the water as she went down, caused by the air bubbles which the craft carried with her in her descent. Only the top of the conning tower was out of water now, the ocean having closed over the deck and the rounded back of the boat. Had any one been watching they would have imagined that an accident was taking place.

In the pilot house, with its thick glass windows, Tom, his father and Captain Weston looked over the surface of the ocean, which every minute was coming nearer and nearer to them.

"We'll be all under in a few seconds," spoke Tom in a solemn voice, as he listened to the water hissing into the tanks.

"Yes, and then we can see what sort of progress we will make," added Mr. Swift. "Everything is going fine, though," he went on cheerfully. "I believe I have a good boat."

"There is no doubt of it in my mind," remarked Captain Weston, and Tom felt a little disappointed that the sailor did not shout out some such expression as "Shiver my timbers!" or "Keel-haul the main braces, there, you lubber!" But Captain Weston was not that kind of a sailor, though his usually quiet demeanor could be quickly dropped on necessity, as Tom learned later.

A few minutes more and the waters closed over the top of the conning tower. The *Advance* was completely submerged. Through the thick glass windows of the pilot house the occupants looked out into the greenish water that swirled about them; but it could not enter. Then, as the boat went lower, the light from above gradually died out, and the semi-darkness gave place to gloom.

"Turn on the electrics and the searchlight, Tom," directed his father.

There was the click of a switch, and the conning tower was flooded with light. But as this had the effect of preventing the three from peering out into the water, just as one in a lighted room cannot look out into the night, Tom shut them off and switched on the great searchlight. This projected its powerful beams straight ahead and there, under the ocean, was a pathway of illumination for the treasure-seekers.

"Fine!" cried Captain Weston, with more enthusiasm than he had yet manifested. "That's great, if you don't mind me mentioning it. How deep are we?"

Tom glanced at a gage on the side of the pilot tower.

"Only about sixty feet," he answered.

"Then don't go any deeper!" cried the captain hastily. "I know these waters around here, and that's about all the depth you've got. You'll be on the bottom in a minute."

"I intend to get on the bottom after a while," said Mr. Swift, "but not here. I want to try for a greater distance under water before I come to rest on the ocean's bed. But I think we are deep enough for a test. Tom, close the tank intake pipes and we'll see how the *Advance* will progress when fully submerged."

The hissing stopped, and then, wishing to see how the motors and other machinery would work, the aged inventor and his son, accompanied by Captain Weston, descended from the conning tower, by means of an inner stairway, to the interior of the ship. The submarine could be steered and managed from below or above. She was now floating about sixty-five feet below the surface of the bay.

"Well, how do you like it?" asked Tom of Mr.

Damon, as he saw his friend in an easy chair in the living-room or main cabin of the craft, looking out of one of the plate-glass windows on the side.

"Bless my spectacles, it's the most wonderful thing I ever dreamed of!" cried the queer character, as he peered at the mass of water before him. "To think that I'm away down under the surface, and yet as dry as a bone. Bless my necktie, but it's great! What are we going to do now?"

"Go forward," replied the young inventor.

"Perhaps I had better make an observation," suggested Captain Weston, taking his telescope from under his arm, where he had carried it since entering the craft, and opening it. "We may run afoul of something, if you don't mind me mentioning such a disagreeable subject." Then, as he thought of the impossibility of using his glass under water, he closed it.

"I shall have little use for this here, I'm afraid," he remarked with a smile. "Well, there's some consolation. We're not likely to meet many ships in this part of the ocean. Other vessels are fond enough of remaining on the surface. I fancy we shall have the depths to ourselves, unless we meet a Government submarine, and they are hardly able to go as deep as we can. No, I guess we won't run into anything and I can put this glass away."

"Unless we run into Berg and his crowd," suggested Tom in a low voice.

"Ha! ha!" laughed Captain Weston, for he did not want Mr. Swift to worry over the unscrupulous agent. "No, I don't believe we'll meet them, Tom. I guess Berg is trying to work out the longitude and latitude I gave him. I wish I could see his face when he realizes that he's been deceived by that fake map."

"Well, I hope he doesn't discover it too soon and trail us," went on the lad. "But they're going to start the machinery now. I suppose you and I had better take charge of the steering of the craft. Dad will want to be in the engine-room."

"All right," replied the captain, and he moved forward with the lad to a small compartment, shut off from the living-room, that served as a pilot house when the conning tower was not used. The same levers, wheels and valves were there as up above, and the submarine could be managed as well from there as from the other place.

"Is everything all right?" asked Mr. Swift as he went into the engine-room, where Garret Jackson and Mr. Sharp were busy with oil cans.

"Everything," replied the balloonist. "Are you going to start now?"

"Yes, we're deep enough for a speed trial. We'll go out to sea, however, and try for a lower depth record, as soon as there's enough water. Start the engine."

A moment later the powerful electric currents were flowing into the forward and aft plates, and the *Advance* began to gather way, forging through the water.

"Straight ahead, out to sea, Tom," called his father to him.

"Aye, aye, sir," responded the youth.

"Ha! Quite seaman-like, if you don't mind a reference to it," commented Captain Weston with a smile. "Mind your helm, boy, for you don't want to poke her nose into a mud bank, or run up on a shoal."

"Suppose you steer?" suggested the lad. "I'd rather take lessons for a while."

"All right. Perhaps it will be safer. I know these waters from the top, though I can't say as much for the bottom. However, I know where the shoals are."

The powerful searchlight was turned, so as to send its beams along the path which the submarine was to follow, and then, as she gathered speed, she shot ahead, gliding through the waters like a fish.

Mr. Damon divided his time between the forward pilot-room, the living-apartment, and the place where Mr. Swift, Garret Jackson and Mr. Sharp were working over the engines. Every few minutes he would bless some part of himself, his clothing, or the ship. Finally the old man settled down to look through the plate-glass windows in the main apartment.

On and on went the submarine. She behaved perfectly, and was under excellent control. Sometimes Tom, at the request of his father, would send her toward the surface by means of the deflecting rudder. Then she would dive to the bottom again. Once, as a test, she was sent obliquely to the surface, her tower just emerging, and then she darted downward again, like a porpoise that had come up to roll over, and suddenly concluded to seek the depths. In fact, had any one seen the maneuver they would have imagined the craft was a big fish disporting itself.

Captain Weston remained at Tom's side, giving him instructions, and watching the compass in order to direct the steering so as to avoid collisions. For an hour or more the craft was sent almost straight ahead at medium speed. Then

Mr. Swift, joining his son and the captain, re-marked:

"How about depth of water here, Captain Weston?"

"You've got more than a mile."

"Good! Then I'm going down to the bottom of the sea! Tom, fill the tanks still more."

"Aye, aye, sir," answered the lad gaily. "Now for a new experience!"

"And use the deflecting rudder, also," advised his father. "That will hasten matters."

Five minutes later there was a slight jar noticeable.

"Bless my soul! What's that?" cried Mr. Damon. "Have we hit something?"

"Yes," answered Tom with a smile.

"What, for gracious sake?"

"The bottom of the sea. We're on the bed of the ocean."

CHAPTER XII

FOR A BREATH OF AIR

THEY could hardly realize it, yet the depth-gage told the story. It registered a distance below the surface of the ocean of five thousand seven hundred feet—a little over a mile. The *Advance* had actually come to rest on the bottom of the Atlantic.

"Hurrah!" cried Tom. "Let's get on the diving suits, dad, and walk about on land under water for a change."

"No," said Mr. Swift soberly. "We will hardly have time for that now. Besides, the suits are not yet fitted with the automatic air-tanks, and we can't use them. There are still some things to do before we start on our treasure cruise. But I want to see how the plates are standing this pressure."

The *Advance* was made with a triple hull, the spaces between the layers of plates being filled with a secret material, capable of withstanding enormous pressure, as were also the plates themselves. Mr. Swift, aided by Mr. Jackson and Captain Weston, made a thorough examination, and found that not a drop of water had leaked in, nor was there the least sign that any of the plates had given way under the terrific strain.

"She's as tight as a drum, if you will allow me to make that comparison," remarked Captain Weston modestly. "I couldn't ask for a dryer ship."

"Well, let's take a look around by means of the searchlight and the observation windows, and then we'll go back," suggested Mr. Swift. "It will take about two days to get the stores and provisions aboard and rig up the diving suits; then we will start for the sunken treasure."

There were several powerful searchlights on the *Advance,* so arranged that the bow, stern or either side could be illuminated independently. There were also observation windows near each light.

In turn the powerful rays were cast first at the bow and then aft. In the gleams could be seen the sandy bed of the ocean, covered with shells of various kinds. Great crabs walked around on their long, jointed legs, and Tom saw some lobsters that would have brought joy to the heart of a fisherman.

"Look at the big fish!" cried Mr. Damon suddenly, and he pointed to some dark, shadowy forms that swam up to the glass windows, evidently puzzled by the light.

"Porpoises," declared Captain Weston briefly. "A whole school of them."

The fish seemed suddenly to multiply, and soon those in the submarine felt curious tremors running through the whole craft.

"The fish are rubbing up against it," cried Tom. "They must think we came down here to allow them to scratch their backs on the steel plates."

For some time they remained on the bottom, watching the wonderful sight of the fishes that swam all about them.

"Well, I think we may as well rise," announced Mr. Swift, after they had been on the bottom about an hour, moving here and there. "We didn't bring any provisions, and I'm getting hungry, though I don't know how the others of you feel about it."

"Bless my dinner-plate, I could eat, too!" cried Mr. Damon. "Go up, by all means. We'll get enough of under-water travel once we start for the treasure."

"Send her up, Tom," called his father. "I want to make a few notes on some needed changes and improvements."

Tom entered the lower pilot house, and turned the valve that opened the tanks. He also pulled the lever that started the pumps, so that the water ballast would be more quickly emptied, as that would render the submarine buoyant, and she would quickly shoot to the surface. To the surprise of the lad, however, there followed no outrushing of the water. The *Advance* remained stationary on the ocean bed. Mr. Swift looked up from his notes.

"Didn't you hear me ask you to send her up, Tom?" he inquired mildly.

"I did, dad, but something seems to be the matter," was the reply.

"Matter? What do you mean?" and the aged inventor hastened to where his son and Captain Weston were at the wheels, valves and levers.

"Why, the tanks won't empty, and the pumps don't seem to work."

"Let me try," suggested Mr. Swift, and he pulled the various handles. There was no corresponding action of the machinery.

"That's odd," he remarked in a curious voice. "Perhaps something has gone wrong with the connections. Go look in the engine-room, and ask Mr. Sharp if everything is all right there."

Tom made a quick trip, returning to report

that the dynamos, motors and gas engine were running perfectly.

"Try to work the tank levers and pumps from the conning tower," suggested Captain Weston. "Sometimes I've known the steam steering gear to play tricks like that."

Tom hurried up the circular stairway into the tower. He pulled the levers and shifted the valves and wheels there. But there was no emptying of the water tanks. The weight and pressure of water in them still held the submarine on the bottom of the sea, more than a mile from the surface. The pumps in the engine-room were working at top speed, but there was evidently something wrong in the connections. Mr. Swift quickly came to this conclusion.

"We must repair it at once," he said. "Tom, come to the engine-room. You and I, with Mr. Jackson and Mr. Sharp, will soon have it in shape again."

"Is there any danger?" asked Mr. Damon in a perturbed voice. "Bless my soul, it's unlucky to have an accident on our trial trip."

"Oh, we must expect accidents," declared Mr. Swift with a smile. "This is nothing."

But it proved to be more difficult than he had imagined to re-establish the connection between the pumps and the tanks. The valves, too, had clogged or jammed, and as the pressure outside the ship was so great, the water would not run out of itself. It must be forced.

For an hour or more the inventor, his son and the others, worked away. They could accomplish nothing. Tom looked anxiously at his parent when the latter paused in his efforts.

"Don't worry," advised the aged inventor. "It's got to come right sooner or later."

Just then Mr. Damon, who had been wandering about the ship, entered the engine-room.

"Do you know," he said, "you ought to open a window, or something."

"Why, what's the matter?" asked Tom quickly, looking to see if the odd man was joking.

"Well, of course I don't exactly mean a window," explained Mr. Damon, "but we need fresh air."

"Fresh air!" There was a startled note in Mr. Swift's voice as he repeated the words.

"Yes, I can hardly breathe in the living-room, and it's not much better here."

"Why, there ought to be plenty of fresh air," went on the inventor. "It is renewed automatically."

Tom jumped up and looked at an indicator. He uttered a startled cry.

"The air hasn't been changed in the last hour!"

he exclaimed. "It is bad. There's not enough oxygen in it. I notice it, now that I've stopped working. The gage indicates it, too. The automatic air-changer must have stopped working. I'll fix it."

He hurried to the machine which was depended on to supply fresh air to the submarine.

"Why, the air tanks are empty!" the young inventor cried. "We haven't any more air except what is in the ship now!"

"And we're rapidly breathing that up," added Captain Weston solemnly.

"Can't you make more?" cried Mr. Damon. "I thought you said you could make oxygen aboard the ship."

"We can," answered Mr. Swift, "but I did not bring along a supply of the necessary chemicals. I did not think we would be submerged long enough for that. But there should have been enough in the reserve tank to last several days. How about it, Tom?"

"It's all leaked out, or else it wasn't filled," was the despairing answer. "All the air we have is what's in the ship, and we can't make more."

The treasure-seekers looked at each other. It was an awful situation.

"Then the only thing to do is to fix the machinery and rise to the surface," said Mr. Sharp simply. "We can have all the air we want, then."

"Yes, but the machinery doesn't seem possible of being fixed," spoke Tom in a low voice.

"We must do it!" cried his father.

They set to work again with fierce energy, laboring for their very lives. They all knew that they could not long remain in the ship without oxygen. Nor could they desert it to go to the surface, for the moment they left the protection of the thick steel sides the terrible pressure of the water would kill them. Nor were the diving suits available. They must stay in the craft and die a miserable death—unless the machinery could be repaired and the *Advance* sent to the surface. The emergency expanding lifting tank was not yet in working order.

More frantically they toiled, trying every device that was suggested to the mechanical minds of Tom, his father, Mr. Sharp or Mr. Jackson, to make the pumps work. But something was wrong. More and more foul grew the air. They were fairly gasping now. It was difficult to breathe, to say nothing of working, in that atmosphere. The thought of their terrible position was in the minds of all.

"Oh, for one breath of fresh air!" cried Mr.

Damon, who seemed to suffer more than any of the others. Grim death was hovering around them, imprisoned as they were on the ocean's bed, over a mile from the surface.

CHAPTER XIII

SUDDENLY Tom, after a moment's pause, seized a wrench and began loosening some nuts.

"What are you doing?" asked his father faintly, for he was being weakened by the vitiated atmosphere.

"I'm going to take this valve apart," replied his son. "We haven't looked there for the trouble. Maybe it's out of order."

He attacked the valve with energy, but his hands soon lagged. The lack of oxygen was telling on him. He could no longer work quickly.

"I'll help," murmured Mr. Sharp thickly. He took a wrench, but no sooner had he loosened one nut than he toppled over. "I'm all in," he murmured feebly.

"Is he dead?" cried Mr. Damon, himself gasping.

"No, only fainted. But he soon will be dead, and so will all of us, if we don't get fresh air," remarked Captain Weston. "Lie down on the floor, every one. There is a little fairly good air there. It's heavier than the air we've breathed, and we can exist on it for a little longer. Poor Sharp was so used to breathing the rarified air of high altitudes that he can't stand this heavy atmosphere."

Mr. Damon was gasping worse than ever, and so was Mr. Swift. The balloonist lay an inert heap on the floor, with Captain Weston trying to force a few drops of stimulant down his throat.

With a fierce determination in his heart, but with fingers that almost refused to do his bidding, Tom once more sought to open the big valve. He felt sure the trouble was located there, as they had tried to locate it in every other place without avail.

"I'll help," said Mr. Jackson in a whisper. He, too, was hardly able to move.

More and more devoid of oxygen grew the air. It gave Tom a sense as if his head was filled, and ready to burst with every breath he drew. Still he struggled to loosen the nuts. There were but four more now, and he took off three while Mr. Jackson removed one. The young inventor lifted off the valve cover, though it felt like a ton weight to him. He gave a glance inside.

"Here's the trouble!" he murmured. "The valve's clogged. No wonder it wouldn't work. The pumps couldn't force the water out."

It was the work of only a minute to adjust the valve. Then Tom and the engineer managed to get the cover back on.

How they inserted the bolts and screwed the nuts in place they never could remember clearly afterward, but they managed it somehow, with shaking, trembling hands and eyes that grew more and more dim.

"Now start the pumps!" cried Tom faintly. "The tanks will be emptied, and we can get to the surface."

Mr. Sharp was still unconscious, nor was Mr. Swift able to help. He lay with his eyes closed. Garret Jackson, however, managed to crawl to the engine-room, and soon the clank of machinery told Tom that the pumps were in motion. The lad staggered to the pilot house and threw the levers over. An instant later there was the hissing of water as it rushed from the ballast tanks. The submarine shivered, as though disliking to leave the bottom of the sea, and then slowly rose. As the pumps worked more rapidly, and the sea was sent from the tank in great volumes, the boat fairly shot to the surface. Tom was ready to open the conning tower and let in fresh air as soon as the top was above the surface.

With a bound the *Advance* reached the top. Tom frantically worked the worm gear that opened the tower. In rushed the fresh, life-giving air, and the treasure-hunters filled their lungs with it.

And it was only just in time, for Mr. Sharp was almost gone. He quickly revived, as did the others, when they could breathe as much as they wished of the glorious oxygen.

"That was a close call," commented Mr. Swift. "We'll not go below again until I have provided for all emergencies. I should have seen to the air tanks and the expanding one before going below. We'll sail home on the surface now."

The submarine was put about and headed for her dock. On the way she passed a small steamer, and the passengers looked down in wonder at the strange craft.

When the *Advance* reached the secluded creek where she had been launched, her passengers had fully recovered from their terrible experience, though the nerves of Mr. Swift and Mr. Damon were not at ease for some days thereafter.

"I should never have made a submerged test without making sure that we had a reserve supply of air," remarked the aged inventor. "I will not be caught that way again. But I can't understand how the pump valve got out of order."

"Maybe some one tampered with it," suggested Mr. Damon. "Could Andy Foger, any of the Happy Harry gang, or the rival gold-seekers have done it?"

"I hardly think so," answered Tom. "The place has been too carefully guarded since Berg and Andy once sneaked in. I think it was just an accident, but I have thought of a plan whereby such accidents can be avoided in the future. It needs a simple device."

"Better patent it," suggested Mr. Sharp with a smile.

"Maybe I will," replied the young inventor. "But not now. We haven't time, if we intend to get fitted out for our trip."

"No; I should say the sooner we started the better," remarked Captain Weston. "That is, if you don't mind me speaking about it," he added gently, and the others smiled, for his diffident comments were only a matter of habit.

The first act of the adventurers, after tying the submarine at the dock, was to proceed with the loading of the food and supplies. Tom and Mr. Damon looked to this, while Mr. Swift and Mr. Sharp made some necessary changes to the machinery. The next day the young inventor at-

tached his device to the pump valve, and the
loading of the craft was continued.

All was in readiness for the gold-seeking expedition a week later. Captain Weston had carefully charted the route they were to follow, and
it was decided to move along on the surface for
the first day, so as to get well out to sea before
submerging the craft. Then it would sink below
the surface, and run along under the water until
the wreck was reached, rising at times, as needed,
to renew the air supply.

With sufficient stores and provisions aboard to
last several months, if necessary, though they did
not expect to be gone more than sixty days at
most, the adventurers arose early one morning
and went down to the dock. Mr. Jackson was
not to accompany them. He did not care about a
submarine trip, he said, and Mr. Swift desired
him to remain at the seaside cottage and guard
the shops, which contained much valuable machinery. The airship was also left there.

"Well, are we all ready?" asked Mr. Swift of
the little party of gold-seekers, as they were about
to enter the conning tower hatchway of the submarine.

"All ready, dad," responded his son.

"Then let's get aboard," proposed Captain
Weston. "But first let me take an observation."

He swept the horizon with his telescope, and Tom noticed that the sailor kept it fixed on one particular spot for some time.

"Did you see anything?" asked the lad.

"Well, there is a boat lying off there," was the answer. "And some one is observing us through a glass. But I don't believe it matters. Probably they're only trying to see what sort of an odd fish we are."

"All aboard, then," ordered Mr. Swift, and they went into the submarine. Tom and his father, with Captain Weston, remained in the conning tower. The signal was given, the electricity flowed into the forward and aft plates, and the *Advance* shot ahead on the surface.

The sailor raised his telescope once more and peered through a window in the tower. He uttered an exclamation.

"What's the matter?" asked Tom.

"That other ship—a small steamer—is weighing anchor and seems to be heading this way," was the reply.

"Maybe it's some one hired by Berg to follow us and trace our movements," suggested Tom.

"If it is we'll fool them," added his father. "Just keep an eye on them, captain, and I think we can show them a trick or two in a few minutes."

Faster shot the *Advance* through the water. She had started on her way to get the gold from the sunken wreck, but already enemies were on the trail of the adventurers, for the ship the sailor had noticed was steaming after them.

CHAPTER XIV

IN THE DIVING SUITS

THERE was no doubt that the steamer was coming after the submarine. Several observations Captain Weston made confirmed this, and he reported the fact to Mr. Swift.

"Well, we'll change our plans, then," said the inventor. "Instead of sailing on the surface we'll go below. But first let them get near so they may have the benefit of seeing what we do. Tom, go below, please, and tell Mr. Sharp to get everything in readiness for a quick descent. I'll slow up a bit now, and let them get nearer to us."

The speed of the submarine was reduced, and in a short time the strange steamer had overhauled her, coming to within hailing distance.

Mr. Swift signaled for the machinery to stop, and the submarine came to a halt on the surface, bobbing about like a half-submerged bottle. The inventor opened a bull's-eye in the tower, and called to a man on the bridge of the steamer:

"What are you following us for?"

"Following you?" repeated the man, for the strange vessel had also come to a stop. "We're not following you."

"It looks like it," replied Mr. Swift. You'd better give it up."

"I guess the waters are free," was the quick retort. "We'll follow you if we like."

"Will you? Then come on!" cried the inventor as he quickly closed the heavy glass window and pulled a lever. An instant later the submarine began to sink, and Mr. Swift could not help laughing as, just before the tower went under water, he had a glimpse of the astonished face of the man on the bridge. The latter had evidently not expected such a move as that.

Lower and lower in the water went the craft, until it was about two hundred feet below the surface. Then Mr. Swift left the conning tower, descended to the main part of the ship, and asked Tom and Captain Weston to take charge of the pilot house.

"Send her ahead, Tom," his father said. "That fellow up above is rubbing his eyes yet, wondering where we are, I suppose."

Forward shot the *Advance* under water, the powerful electrical plates pulling and pushing her on the way to secure the sunken gold.

All that morning a fairly moderate rate of speed was maintained, as it was thought best not to run the new machinery too fast.

Dinner was eaten about a quarter of a mile below the surface, but no one inside the submarine would ever have known it. Electric lights made the place as brilliant as could be desired, and the food, which Tom and Mr. Damon prepared, was equal to any that could have been served on land. After the meal they opened the shutters over the windows in the sides of the craft, and looked at the myriads of fishes swimming past, as the creatures were disclosed in the glare of the searchlight.

That night they were several hundred miles on their journey, for the craft was speedy, and leaving Tom and Captain Weston to take the first watch, the others went to bed.

"Bless my soul, but it does seem odd, though, to go to bed under water, like a fish," remarked Mr. Damon. "If my wife knew this she would worry to death. She thinks I'm off automobiling. But this isn't half as dangerous as riding in a car that's always getting out of order. A submarine for mine, every time."

"Wait until we get to the end of this trip," advised Tom. "I guess you'll find almost as many things can happen in a submarine as can in an auto," and future events were to prove the young inventor to be right.

Everything worked well that night, and the ship made good progress. They rose to the surface the next morning to make sure of their position, and to get fresh air, though they did not really need the latter, as the reserve supply had not been drawn on, and was sufficient for several days, now that the oxygen machine had been put in running order.

On the second day the ship was sent to the bottom and halted there, as Mr. Swift wished to try the new diving suits. These were made of a new, light, but very strong metal to withstand the pressure of a great depth.

Tom, Mr. Sharp and Captain Weston donned the suits, the others agreeing to wait until they saw how the first trial resulted. Then, too, it was necessary for some one acquainted with the machinery to remain in the ship to operate the door and water chamber through which the divers had to pass to get out.

The usual plan, with some changes, was followed in letting the three out of the boat, and on to the bottom of the sea. They entered a chamber in the side of the submarine, water was gradually admitted until it equaled in pressure that outside, then an outer door was opened by means of levers, and they could step out.

It was a curious sensation to Tom and the others to feel that they were actually walking along the bed of the ocean. All around them was the water, and as they turned on the small electric lights in their helmets, which lights were fed by storage batteries fastened to the diving suits, they saw the fish, big and little, swarm up to them, doubtless astonished at the odd creatures which had entered their domain. On the sand of the bottom, and in and out among the shells and rocks, crawled great spider crabs, big eels and other odd creatures seldom seen on the surface of the water. The three divers found no difficulty in breathing, as there were air tanks fastened to their shoulders, and a constant supply of oxygen was fed through pipes into the helmets. The pressure of water did not bother them, and after the first sensation Tom began to enjoy the novelty of it. At first the inability to speak to his companions seemed odd, but he soon got so he could make signs and motions, and be understood.

They walked about for some time, and once the lad came upon a part of a wrecked vessel buried deep in the sand. There was no telling what ship it was, nor how long it had been there, and after silently viewing it, they continued on.

"It was great!" were the first words Tom uttered when he and the others were once more inside the submarine and had removed the suits. "If we can only walk around the wreck of the *Boldero* that way, we'll have all the gold out of her in no time. There are no life-lines nor air-hose to bother with in these diving suits."

"They certainly are a success," conceded Mr. Sharp.

"Bless my topknot!" cried Mr. Damon. "I'll try it next time. I've always wanted to be a diver, and now I have the chance."

The trip was resumed after the diving chamber had been closed, and on the third day Captain Weston announced, after a look at his chart, that they were nearing the Bahama Islands.

"We'll have to be careful not to run into any of the small keys," he said, that being the name for the many little points of land, hardly large enough to be dignified by the name of island. "We must keep a constant lookout."

Fortune favored them, though once, when Tom was steering, he narrowly evoided ramming a coral reef with the submarine. The searchlight showed it to him just in time, and he sheered off with a thumping in his heart.

The course was changed from south to east, so as to get ready to swing out of the way of the big shoulder of South America where Brazil takes up so much room, and as they went farther and farther toward the equator, they noticed that the waters teemed more and more with fish, some beautiful, some ugly and fear-inspiring, and some such monsters that it made one shudder to look at them, even through the thick glass of the bull's-eye windows.

CHAPTER XV

AT THE TROPICAL ISLAND

IT was on the evening of the fourth day later that Captain Weston, who was steering the craft, suddenly called out:

"Land ho!"

"Where away?" inquired Tom quickly, for he had read that this was the proper response to make.

"Dead ahead," answered the sailor with a smile. "Shall we make for it, if I may be allowed the question?"

"What land is it likely to be?" Mr. Swift wanted to know.

"Oh, some small tropical island," replied the seafaring man. "It isn't down on the charts. Probably it's too small to note. I should say it was a coral island, but we may be able to find a spring of fresh water there, and some fruit."

"Then we'll land there," decided the inventor.

"We can use some fresh water, though our distilling and ice apparatus does very well."

They made the island just at dusk, and anchored in a little lagoon, where there was a good depth of water.

"Now for shore!" cried Tom, as the submarine swung around on the chain. "It looks like a fine place. I hope there are cocoanuts and oranges here. Shall I get out the electric launch, dad?"

"Yes, you may, and we'll all go ashore. It will do us good to stretch our legs a bit."

Carried in a sort of pocket on the deck of the submarine was a small electric boat, capable of holding six. It could be slid from the pocket, or depression, into the water without the use of davits, and, with Mr. Sharp to aid him, Tom soon had the little craft afloat. The batteries were already charged, and just as the sun was going down the gold-seekers entered the launch and were soon on shore.

They found a good spring of water close at hand, and Tom's wish regarding the cocoanuts was realized, though there were no oranges. The lad took several of the delicious nuts, and breaking them open poured the milk into a collapsible cup he carried, drinking it eagerly. The others followed his example, and pronounced it the best beverage they had tasted in a long time.

The island was a typical tropical one, not very large, and it did not appear to have been often visited by man. There were no animals to be seen, but myriads of birds flew here and there amid the trees, the trailing vines and streamers of moss.

"Let's spend a day here to-morrow and explore it," proposed Tom, and his father nodded an assent. They went back to the submarine as night was beginning to gather, and in the cabin, after supper, talked over the happenings of their trip so far.

"Do you think we'll have any trouble getting the gold out of the wrecked vessel?" asked Tom of Captain Weston, after a pause.

"Well, it's hard to say. I couldn't learn just how the wreck lays, whether it's on a sandy or a rocky bottom. If the latter, it won't be so hard, but if the sand has worked in and partly covered it, we'll have some difficulties, if I may be permitted to say so. However, don't borrow trouble. We're not there yet, though at the rate we're traveling it won't be long before we arrive."

No watch was set that night, as it was not considered necessary. Tom was the first to arise in the morning, and he went out on the deck for a breath of fresh air before breakfast.

He looked off at the beautiful little island, and as his eye took in all of the little lagoon where the submarine was anchored he uttered a startled cry.

And well he might, for, not a hundred yards away, and nearer to the island than was the *Advance,* floated another craft—another craft, almost similar in shape and size to the one built by the Swifts. Tom rubbed his eyes to make sure he was not seeing double. No, there could be no mistake about it. There was another submarine at the tropical island.

As he looked, some one emerged from the conning tower of the second craft. The figure seemed strangely familiar. Tom knew in a moment who it was—Addison Berg. The agent saw the lad, too, and taking off his cap and making a mocking bow, he called out:

"Good morning! Have you got the gold yet?"

Tom did not know what to answer. Seeing the other submarine, at an island where he had supposed they would not be disturbed, was disconcerting enough, but to be greeted by Berg was altogether too much, Tom thought. His fears that the rival boat builders would follow had not been without foundation.

"Rather surprised to see us, aren't you?" went on Mr. Berg, smiling.

"Rather," admitted Tom, choking over the word.

"Thought you'd be," continued Berg. "We didn't expect to meet you so soon, but we're glad we did. I don't altogether like hunting for sunken treasure, with such indefinite directions as I have."

"You—are going to——" stammered Tom, and then he concluded it would be best not to say anything. But his talk had been heard inside the submarine. His father came to the foot of the conning tower stairway.

"To whom are you speaking, Tom?" he asked.

"They're here, dad," was the youth's answer.

"Here? Who are here?"

"Berg and his employers. They've followed us, dad."

CHAPTER XVI

"WE'LL RACE YOU FOR IT"

Mr. Swift hurried up on deck. He was accompanied by Captain Weston. At the sight of Tom's father, Mr. Berg, who had been joined by two other men, called out:

"You see we also concluded to give up the trial for the Government prize, Mr. Swift. We decided there was more money in something else. But we still will have a good chance to try the merits of our respective boats. We hurried and got ours fitted up almost as soon as you did yours, and I think we have the better craft."

"I don't care to enter into any competition with you," said Mr. Swift coldly.

"Ah, but I'm afraid you'll have to, whether you want to or not," was the insolent reply.

"What's that? Do you mean to force this matter upon me?"

"I'm afraid I'll have to—my employers and I, that is. You see, we managed to pick up your trail after you left the Jersey coast, having an idea where you were bound, and we don't intend to lose you now."

"Do you mean to follow us?" asked Captain Weston softly.

"Well, you can put it that way if you like," answered one of the two men with Mr. Berg.

"I forbid it!" cried Mr. Swift hotly. "You have no right to sneak after us."

"I guess the ocean is free," continued the rascally agent.

"Why do you persist in keeping after us?" inquired the aged inventor, thinking it well to ascertain, if possible, just how much the men knew."

"Because we're after that treasure as well as you," was the bold reply. "You have no exclusive right to it. The sunken ship is awaiting the first comer, and whoever gets there first can take the gold from the wreck. We intend to be there first, but we'll be fair with you."

"Fair? What do you mean?" demanded Tom.

"This: We'll race you for it. The first one to arrive will have the right to search the wreck for the gold bullion. Is that fair? Do you agree to it?"

"We agree to nothing with you," interrupted Captain Weston, his usual diffident manner all gone. "I happen to be in partial command of this craft, and I warn you that if I find you interfering with us it won't be healthy for you. I'm not fond of fighting, but when I begin I don't like to stop," and he smiled grimly. "You'd better not follow us."

"We'll do as we please," shouted the third member of the trio on the deck of the other boat, which, as Tom could see, was named the *Wonder.* "We intend to get that gold if we can."

"All right. I've warned you," went on the sailor, and then, motioning to Tom and his father to follow, he went below.

"Well, what's to be done?" asked Mr. Swift when they were seated in the living-room, and had informed the others of the presence of the rival submarine.

"The only thing I see to do is to sneak away unobserved, go as deep as possible, and make all haste for the wreck," advised the captain. "They will depend on us, for they have evidently no chart of the wreck, though of course the general location of it may be known to them from reading the papers. I hoped I had thrown them off the track by the false chart I dropped, but it seems they were too smart for us."

"Have they a right to follow us?" asked Tom.

"Legally, but not morally. We can't prevent

them, I'm afraid. The only thing to do is to get there ahead of them. It will be a race for the sunken treasure, and we must get there first."

"What do you propose doing, captain?" asked Mr. Damon. "Bless my shirt-studs, but can't we pull their ship up on the island and leave it there?"

"I'm afraid such high-handed proceedings would hardly answer," replied Mr. Swift. "No, as Captain Weston says, we must get there ahead of them. What do you think will be the best scheme, captain?"

"Well, there's no need for us to forego our plan to get fresh water. Suppose we go to the island, that is, some of us, leaving a guard on board here. We'll fill our tanks with fresh water, and at night we'll quietly sink below the surface and speed away."

They all voted that an excellent idea, and little time was lost putting it into operation.

All the remainder of that day not a sign of life was visible about the *Wonder*. She lay inert on the surface of the lagoon, not far away from the *Advance;* but, though no one showed himself on the deck, Tom and his friends had no doubt but that their enemies were closely watching them.

As dusk settled down over the tropical sea, and as the shadows of the trees on the little island

lengthened, those on board the *Advance* closed
the conning tower. No lights were turned on,
as they did not want their movements to be seen,
but Tom, his father and Mr. Sharp took their
positions near the various machines and apparatus,
ready to open the tanks and let the submarine
sink to the bottom, as soon as it was possible to
do this unobserved.

"Luckily there's no moon," remarked Captain
Weston, as he took his place beside Tom. "Once
below the surface and we can defy them to find
us. It is odd how they traced us, but I suppose
that steamer gave them the clue."

It rapidly grew dark, as it always does in the
tropics, and when a cautious observation from
the conning tower did not disclose the outlines of
the other boat, those aboard the *Advance* rightly
concluded that their rivals were unable to see
them.

"Send her down, Tom," called his father, and
with a hiss the water entered the tanks. The
submarine quickly sank below the surface, aided
by the deflecting rudder.

But alas for the hopes of the gold-seekers. No
sooner was she completely submerged, with the
engine started so as to send her out of the lagoon
and to the open sea, than the waters all about
were made brilliant by the phosphorescent phe-

nomenon. In southern waters this frequently
occurs. Millions of tiny creatures, which, it is
said, swarm in the warm currents, give an appearance of fire to the ocean, and any object moving through it can plainly be seen. It was so
with the *Advance*. The motion she made in
shooting forward, and the undulations caused by
her submersion, seemed to start into activity the
dormant phosphorus, and the submarine was afloat
in a sea of fire.

"Quick!" cried Tom. "Speed her up! Maybe
we can get out of this patch of water before they
see us."

But it was too late. Above them they could
hear the electric siren of the *Wonder* as it was
blown to let them know that their escape had
been noticed. A moment later the water, which
acted as a sort of sounding-board, or telephone,
brought to the ears of Tom Swift and his friends
the noise of the engines of the other craft in
operation. She was coming after them. The
race for the possession of three hundred thousand dollars in gold was already under way.
Fate seemed against those on board the *Advance*.

CHAPTER XVII

THE RACE

DIRECTED by Captain Weston, who glanced at the compass and told him which way to steer to clear the outer coral reef, Tom sent the submarine ahead, signaling for full speed to the engine-room, where his father and Mr. Sharp were. The big dynamos purred like great cats, as they sent the electrical energy into the forward and aft plates, pulling and pushing the *Advance* forward. On and on she rushed under water, but ever as she shot ahead the disturbance in the phosphor-escent water showed her position plainly. She would be easy to follow.

"Can't you get any more speed out of her?" asked the captain of the lad.

"Yes," was the quick reply; "by using the auxiliary screws I think we can. I'll try it."

He signaled for the propellers, forward and aft, to be put in operation, and the motor moving the twin screws was turned on. At once there was a perceptible increase to the speed of the *Advance*.

"Are we leaving them behind?" asked Tom anxiously, as he glanced at the speed gage, and noted that the submarine was now about five hundred feet below the surface.

"Hard to tell," replied the captain. "You'd have to take an observation to make sure."

"I'll do it," cried the youth. "You steer, please, and I'll go in the conning tower. I can look forward and aft there, as well as straight up. Maybe I can see the *Wonder*."

Springing up the circular ladder leading into the tower, Tom glanced through the windows all about the small pilot house. He saw a curious sight. It was as if the submarine was in a sea of yellowish liquid fire. She was immersed in water which glowed with the flames that contained no heat. So light was it, in fact, that there was no need of the incandescents in the tower. The young inventor could have seen to read a paper by the illumination of the phosphorus. But he had something else to do than observe this phenomenon. He wanted to see if he could catch sight of the rival submarine.

At first he could make out nothing save the swirl and boiling of the sea, caused by the progress of the *Advance* through it. But suddenly, as he looked up, he was aware of some great, black body a little to the rear and about ten feet above his craft.

"A shark!" he exclaimed aloud. "An immense one, too."

But the closer he looked the less it seemed like a shark. The position of the black object changed. It appeared to settle down, to be approaching the top of the conning tower. Then, with a suddenness that unnerved him for the time being, Tom recognized what it was; it was the underside of a ship. He could see the plates riveted together, and then, as he noted the rounded, cylindrical shape, he knew that it was a submarine. It was the *Wonder*. She was close at hand and was creeping up on the *Advance*. But, what was more dangerous, she seemed to be slowly settling in the water. Another moment and her great screws might crash into the conning tower of the Swifts' boat and shave it off. Then the water would rush in, drowning the treasure-seekers like rats in a trap.

With a quick motion Tom yanked over the lever that allowed more water to flow into the ballast tanks. The effect was at once apparent. The *Advance* shot down toward the bottom of the sea. At the same time the young inventor signaled to Captain Weston to notify those in the engine-room to put on a little more speed. The *Advance* fairly leaped ahead, and the lad, looking up through the bull's-eye in the roof of the conning tower, had the satisfaction of seeing the rival submarine left behind.

The youth hurried down into the interior of the ship to tell what he had seen, and explain the reason for opening the ballast tanks. He found his father and Mr. Sharp somewhat excited over the unexpected maneuver of the craft.

"So they're still following us," murmured Mr. Swift. "I don't see why we can't shake them off."

"It's on account of this luminous water," explained Captain Weston. "Once we are clear of that it will be easy, I think, to give them the slip. That is, if we can get out of their sight long enough. Of course, if they keep close after us, they can pick us up with their searchlight, for I suppose they carry one."

"Yes," admitted the aged inventor, "they have as strong a one as we have. In fact, their ship is second only to this one in speed and power. I know, for Bentley & Eagert showed me some of the plans before they started it, and asked my opinion. This was before I had the notion of building a submarine. Yes, I am afraid we'll have trouble getting away from them."

"I can't understand this phosphorescent glow keeping up so long," remarked Captain Weston. "I've seen it in this locality several times, but it never covered such an extent of the ocean in my time. There must be changed conditions here now."

For an hour or more the race was kept up, and the two submarines forged ahead through the glowing sea. The *Wonder* remained slightly above and to the rear of the other, the better to keep sight of her, and though the *Advance* was run to her limit of speed, her rival could not be shaken off. Clearly the *Wonder* was a speedy craft.

"It's too bad that we've got to fight them, as well as run the risk of lots of other troubles which are always present when sailing under water," observed Mr. Damon, who wandered about the submarine like the nervous person he was. "Bless my shirt-studs! Can't we blow them up, or cripple them in some way? They have no right to go after our treasure."

"Well, I guess they've got as much right as we have," declared Tom. "It goes to whoever reaches the wreck first. But what I don't like is their mean, sneaking way of doing it. If they went off on their own hook and looked for it I wouldn't say a word. But they expect us to lead them to the wreck, and then they'll rob us if they can. That's not fair."

"Indeed, it isn't," agreed Captain Weston, "if I may be allowed the expression. We ought to find some way of stopping them. But, if I'm not mistaken," he added quickly, looking from one of the port bull's-eyes, "the phosphorescent glow is lessening. I believe we are running beyond that part of the ocean."

There was no doubt of it, the glow was growing less and less, and ten minutes later the *Advance* was speeding along through a sea as black as night. Then, to avoid running into some wreck, it was necessary to turn on the searchlight.

"Are they still after us?" asked Mr. Swift of his son, as he emerged from the engine-room, where he had gone to make some adjustments to the machinery, with the hope of increasing the speed.

"I'll go look," volunteered the lad. He climbed up into the conning tower again, and for a moment, as he gazed back into the black waters swirling all about, he hoped that they had lost the *Wonder*. But a moment later his heart sank as he caught sight, through the liquid element, of the flickering gleams of another searchlight, the rays undulating through the sea.

"Still following," murmured the young inventor. "They're not going to give up. But we must make 'em—that's all."

He went down to report what he had seen, and a consultation was held. Captain Weston carefully studied the charts of that part of the ocean, and finding that there was a great depth of water at hand, proposed a series of evolutions.

"We can go up and down, shoot first to one side and then to the other," he explained. "We can even drop down to the bottom and rest there for a while. Perhaps, in that way, we can shake them off."

They tried it. The *Advance* was sent up until her conning tower was out of the water, and then she was suddenly forced down until she was but a few feet from the bottom. She darted to the left, to the right, and even doubled and went back over the course she had taken. But all to no purpose. The *Wonder* proved fully as speedy, and those in her seemed to know just how to handle the submarine, so that every evolution of the *Advance* was duplicated. Her rival could not be shaken off.

All night this was kept up, and when morning came, though only the clocks told it, for eternal night was below the surface, the rival gold-seekers were still on the trail.

"They won't give up," declared Mr. Swift hopelessly.

"No, we've got to race them for it, just as Berg proposed," admitted Tom. "But if they want a straightaway race we'll give it to 'em. Let's run her to the limit, dad."

"That's what we've been doing, Tom."

"No, not exactly, for we've been submerged a little too much to get the best speed out of our craft. Let's go a little nearer the surface, and give them the best race they'll ever have."

Then the race began; and such a contest of speed as it was! With her propellers working to the limit, and every volt of electricity that was available forced into the forward and aft plates, the *Advance* surged through the water, about ten feet below the surface. But the *Wonder* kept after her, giving her knot for knot. The course of the leading submarine was easy to trace now, in the morning light which penetrated ten feet down.

"No use," remarked Tom again, when, after two hours, the *Wonder* was still close behind them. "Our only chance is that they may have a breakdown."

"Or run out of air, or something like that," added Captain Weston. "They are crowding us pretty close. I had no idea they could keep up this speed. If they don't look out," he went on as he looked from one of the aft observation windows, "they'll foul us, and——"

His remarks were interrupted by a jar to the *Advance*. She seemed to shiver and careened to one side. Then came another bump.

"Slow down!" cried the captain, rushing toward the pilot house.

"What's the matter?" asked Tom, as he threw the engines and electrical machines out of gear. Have we hit anything?"

"No. Something has hit us," cried the captain. "Their submarine has rammed us."

"Rammed us!" repeated Mr. Swift. "Tom, run out the electric cannon! They're trying to sink us! We'll have to fight them. Run out the stern electric gun and we'll make them wish they'd not followed us!"

CHAPTER XVIII

THE ELECTRIC GUN

THERE was much excitement aboard the *Advance*. The submarine came to a stop in the water, while the treasure-seekers waited anxiously for what was to follow. Would they be rammed again? This time, stationary as they were, and with the other boat coming swiftly on, a hole might be stove through the *Advance,* in spite of her powerful sides.

They had not long to wait. Again there came a jar, and once more the Swifts' boat careened. But the blow was a glancing one and, fortunately, did little damage.

"They certainly must be trying to sink us," agreed Captain Weston. "Come, Tom, we'll take a look from the stern and see what they're up to."

"And get the stern electric gun ready to fire," repeated Mr. Swift. "We must protect ourselves. Mr. Sharp and I will go to the bow. There is no telling what they may do. They're desperate, and may ram us from in front."

Tom and the captain hurried aft. Through the thick plate-glass windows they could see the blunt nose of the *Wonder* not far away, the rival submarine having come to a halt. There she lay, black and silent, like some monster fish waiting to devour its victim.

"There doesn't appear to be much damage done back here," observed Tom. "No leaks. Guess they didn't puncture us."

"Perhaps it was due to an accident that they rammed us," suggested the captain.

"Well, they wouldn't have done it if they hadn't followed us so close," was the opinion of the young inventor. "They're taking too many chances. We've got to stop 'em."

"What is this electric gun your father speaks of?"

"Why, it's a regular electric cannon. It fires a solid ball, weighing about twenty-five pounds, but instead of powder, which would hardly do under water, and instead of compressed air, which is used in the torpedo tubes of the Government submarines, we use a current of electricity. It forces the cannon ball out with great energy."

"I wonder what they will do next?" observed the captain, peering through a bull's-eye.

"We can soon tell," replied the youth. "We'll go ahead, and if they try to follow I'm going to fire on them."

"Suppose you sink them?"

"I won't fire to do that; only to disable them. They brought it on themselves. We can't risk having them damage us. Help me with the cannon, will you please, captain?"

The electric cannon was a long, steel tube in the after part of the submarine. It projected a slight distance from the sides of the ship, and by an ingenious arrangement could be swung around in a ball and socket joint, thus enabling it to shoot in almost any direction.

It was the work of but a few minutes to get it ready and, with the muzzle pointing toward the *Wonder,* Tom adjusted the electric wires and inserted the solid shot.

"Now we're prepared for them!" he cried. "I think a good plan will be to start ahead, and if they try to follow to fire on them. They've brought it on themselves."

"Correct," spoke Captain Weston.

Tom hurried forward to tell his father of this plan.

"We'll do it!" cried Mr. Swift. "Go ahead, Mr. Sharp, and we'll see if those scoundrels will follow."

The young inventor returned on the run to the electric cannon. There was a whirr of machinery, and the *Advance* moved forward. She increased her speed, and the two watchers in the stern loked anxiously out of the windows to see what their rivals would do.

For a moment no movement was noticeable on the part of the *Wonder*. Then, as those aboard her appeared to realize that the craft on which they depended to pilot them to the sunken treasure was slipping away, word was given to follow. The ship of Berg and his employers shot after the *Advance*.

"Here they come!" cried Captain Weston. "They're going to ram us again!"

"Then I'm going to fire on them!" declared Tom savagely.

On came the *Wonder,* nearer and nearer. Her speed was rapidly increasing. Suddenly she bumped the *Advance,* and then, as if it was an unavoidable accident, the rear submarine sheered off to one side.

"They're certainly at it again!" cried Tom, and peering from the bull's-eye he saw the *Wonder* shoot past mouth of the electric cannon. "Here it goes!" he added.

He shoved over the lever, making the proper connection. There was no corresponding report, for the cannon was noiseless, but there was a slight jar as the projectile left the muzzle. The *Wonder* could be seen to heel over.

"You hit her! You hit her!" cried Captain Weston. "A good shot!"

"I was afraid she was past me when I pulled the lever," explained Tom. "She went like a flash."

"No, you caught her on the rudder," declared the captain. "I think you've put her out of business. Yes, they're rising to the surface."

The lad rapidly inserted another ball, and recharged the cannon. Then he peered out into the water, illuminated by the light of day overhead, as they were not far down. He could see the *Wonder* rising to the surface. Clearly something had happened.

"Maybe they're going to drop down on us from above, and try to sink us," suggested the youth, while he stood ready to fire again. "If they do——"

His words were interrupted by a slight jar throughout the submarine.

"What was that?" cried the captain.

"Dad fired the bow gun at them, but I don't believe he hit them," answered the young inventor. "I wonder what damage I did? Guess we'll go to the surface to find out."

Clearly the *Wonder* had given up the fight for the time being. In fact, she had no weapon with which to respond to a fusilade from her rival. Tom hastened forward and informed his father of what had happened.

"If her steering gear is out of order, we may have a chance to slip away," said Mr. Swift. "We'll go up and see what we can learn."

A few minutes later Tom, his father and Captain Weston stepped from the conning tower, which was out of water, on to the little flat deck. A short distance away lay the *Wonder,* and on her deck was Berg and a number of men, evidently members of the crew.

"Why did you fire on us?" shouted the agent angrily.

"Why did you follow us?" retorted Tom.

"Well, you've broken our rudder and disabled us," went on Berg, not answering the question. "You'll suffer for this! I'll have you arrested."

"You only got what you deserved," added Mr. Swift. "You were acting illegally, following us, and you tried to sink us by ramming my craft, before we retaliated by firing on you."

"It was an accident, ramming you," said Berg. "We couldn't help it. I now demand that you help us make repairs."

"Well, you've got nerve!" cried Captain

Weston, his eyes flashing. "I'd like to have a personal interview with you for about ten minutes. Maybe something besides your ship would need repairs then."

Berg turned away, scowling, but did not reply. He began directing the crew what to do about the broken rudder.

"Come on," proposed Tom in a low voice, for sounds carry very easily over water. "Let's go below and skip out while we have a chance. They can't follow now, and we can get to the sunken treasure ahead of them."

"Good advice," commented his father. "Come, Captain Weston, we'll go below and close the conning tower."

Five minutes later the *Advance* sank from sight, the last glimpse Tom had of Berg and his men being a sight of them standing on the deck of their floating boat, gazing in the direction of their successful rival. The *Wonder* was left behind, while Tom and his friends were soon once more speeding toward the treasure wreck.

CHAPTER XIX

CAPTURED

"Down deep," advised Captain Weston, as he stood beside Tom and Mr. Swift in the pilot house. "As far as you can manage her, and then forward. We'll take no more chances with these fellows."

"The only trouble is," replied the young inventor, "that the deeper we go the slower we have to travel. The water is so dense that it holds us back."

"Well, there is no special need of hurrying now," went on the sailor. "No one is following you, and two or three days difference in reaching the wreck will not amount to anything."

"Unless they repair their rudder, and take after us again," suggested Mr. Swift.

"They're not very likely to do that," was the captain's opinion. "It was more by luck than good management that they picked us up before. Now, having to delay, as they will, to repair their

156

steering gear, while we can go as deep as we please and speed ahead, it is practically impossible for them to catch up to us. No, I think we have nothing to fear from them."

But though danger from Berg and his crowd was somewhat remote, perils of another sort were hovering around the treasure-seekers, and they were soon to experience them.

It was much different from sailing along in the airship, Tom thought, for there was no blue sky and fleecy clouds to see, and they could not look down and observe, far below them, cities and villages. Nor could they breathe the bracing atmosphere of the upper regions.

But if there was lack of the rarefied air of the clouds, there was no lack of fresh atmosphere. The big tanks carried a large supply, and whenever more was needed the oxygen machine would supply it.

As there was no need, however, of remaining under water for any great stretch of time, it was their practice to rise every day and renew the air supply, also to float along on the surface for a while, or speed along, with only the conning tower out, in order to afford a view, and to enable Captain Weston to take observations. But care was always exercised to make sure no ships were in sight when emerging on the surface, for the gold-seekers did not want to be hailed and questioned by inquisitive persons.

It was about four days after the disabling of the rival submarine, and the *Advance* was speeding along about a mile and a half under water. Tom was in the pilot house with Captain Weston, Mr. Damon was at his favorite pastime of looking out of the glass side windows into the ocean and its wonders, and Mr. Swift and the balloonists were, as usual, in the engine-room.

"How near do you calculate we are to the sunken wreck?" asked Tom of his companion.

"Well, at the calculation we made yesterday, we are within about a thousand miles of it now. We ought to reach it in about four more days, if we don't have any accidents."

"And how deep do you think it is?" went on the lad.

"Well, I'm afraid it's pretty close to two miles, if not more. It's quite a depth, and of course impossible for ordinary divers to reach. But it will be possible in this submarine and in the strong diving suits your father has invented for us to get to it. Yes, I don't anticipate much trouble in getting out the gold, once we reach the wreck. Of course——"

The captain's remark was not finished. From the engine-room there came a startled shout:

"Tom! Tom! Your father is hurt! Come here, quick!"

"Take the wheel!" cried the lad to the captain. "I must go to my father." It was Mr. Sharp's voice he had heard.

Racing to the engine-room, Tom saw his parent doubled up over a dynamo, while to one side, his hand on a copper switch, stood Mr. Sharp.

"What's the matter?" shouted the lad.

"He's held there by a current of electricity," replied the balloonist. "The wires are crossed."

"Why don't you shut off the current?" demanded the youth, as he prepared to pull his parent from the whirring machine. Then he hesitated, for he feared he, too, would be glued fast by the terrible current, and so be unable to help Mr. Swift.

"I'm held fast here, too," replied the balloonist. "I started to cut out the current at this switch, but there's a short circuit somewhere, and I can't let go, either. Quick, shut off all power at the main switchboard forward."

Tom realized that this was the only thing to do. He ran forward and with a yank cut out all the electric wires. With a sigh of relief Mr. Sharp pulled his hands from the copper where he had been held fast as if by some powerful magnet, his muscles cramped by the current. Fortunately the electricity was of low voltage, and he was not burned. The body of Mr. Swift toppled backward from the dynamo, as Tom sprang to reach his father.

"He's dead!" he cried, as he saw the pale face and the closed eyes.

"No, only badly shocked, I hope," spoke Mr. Sharp. "But we must get him to the fresh air at once. Start the tank pumps. We'll rise to the surface."

The youth needed no second bidding. Once more turning on the electric current, he set the powerful pumps in motion and the submarine began to rise. Then, aided by Captain Weston and Mr. Damon, the young inventor carried his father to a couch in the main cabin. Mr. Sharp took charge of the machinery.

Restoratives were applied, and there was a flutter of the eyelids of the aged inventor.

"I think he'll come around all right," said the sailor kindly, as he saw Tom's grief. "Fresh air will be the thing for him. We'll be on the surface in a minute."

Up shot the *'Advance,* while Mr. Sharp stood ready to open the conning tower as soon as it should be out of water. Mr. Swift seemed to be rapidly reviving. With a bound the submarine, forced upward from the great depth, fairly shot out of the water. There was a clanking sound as the aeronaut opened the airtight door of the tower, and a breath of fresh air came in.

"Can you walk, dad, or shall we carry you?" asked Tom solitiously.

"Oh, I—I'm feeling better now," was the inventor's reply. "I'll soon be all right when I get out on deck. My foot slipped as I was adjusting a wire that had gotten out of order, and I fell so that I received a large part of the current. I'm glad I was not burned. Was Mr. Sharp hurt? I saw him run to the switch, just before I lost consciousness."

"No, I'm all right," answered the balloonist. "But allow us to get you out to the fresh air. You'll feel much better then."

Mr. Swift managed to walk slowly to the ladder leading to the conning tower, and thence to the deck. The others followed him. As all emerged from the submarine they uttered a cry of astonishment.

There, not one hundred yards away, was a great warship, flying a flag which, in a moment, Tom recognized as that of Brazil. The cruiser was lying off a small island, and all about were small boats, filled with natives, who seemed to be bringing supplies from land to the ship. At the unexpected sight of the submarine, bobbing up from the bottom of the ocean, the natives uttered cries of fright. The attention of those on the warship was attracted, and the bridge and rails were lined with curious officers and men.

"It's a good thing we didn't come up under that ship," observed Tom. "They would have thought we were trying to torpedo her. Do you feel better, dad?" he asked, his wonder over the sight of the big vessel temporarily eclipsed in his anxiety for his parent.

"Oh, yes, much better. I'm all right now. But I wish we hadn't disclosed ourselves to these people. They may demand to know where we are going, and Brazil is too near Uruguay to make it safe to tell our errand. They may guess it, however, from having read of the wreck, and our departure."

"Oh, I guess it will be all right," replied Captain Weston. "We can tell them we are on a pleasure trip. That's true enough. It would give us great pleasure to find that gold."

"There's a boat, with some officers in it, to judge by the amount of gold lace on them, putting off from the ship," remarked Mr. Sharp.

"Ha! Yes! Evidently they intend to pay us a formal visit," observed Mr. Damon. "Bless my gaiters, though. I'm not dressed to receive company. I think I'll put on my dress suit."

"It's too late," advised Tom. "They'll be here in a minute."

Urged on by the lusty arms of the Brazilian sailors, the boat, containing several officers, neared the floating submarine rapidly.

"Ahoy there!" called an officer in the bow, his accent betraying his unfamiliarity with the English language. "What craft are you?"

"Submarine, *Advance,* from New Jersey," replied Tom. "Who are you?"

"Brazilian cruiser *San Paulo,*" was the reply. "Where are you bound?" went on the officer.

"On pleasure," answered Captain Weston quickly. "But why do you ask? We are an American ship, sailing under American colors. Is this Brazilian territory?"

"This island is—yes," came back the answer, and by this time the small boat was at the side of the submarine. Before the adventurers could have protested, had they a desire to do so, there were a number of officers and the crew of the *San Paulo* on the small deck.

With a flourish, the officer who had done the questioning drew his sword. Waving it in the air with a dramatic gesture, he exclaimed:

"You're our prisoners! Resist and my men shall cut you down like dogs! Seize them, men!"

The sailors sprang forward, each one stationing himself at the side of one of our friends, and grasping an arm.

"What does this mean?" cried Captain Weston indignantly. "If this is a joke, you're carrying it too far. If you're in earnest, let me warn you against interfering with Americans!"

"We know what we are doing," was the answer from the officer.

The sailor who had hold of Captain Weston endeavored to secure a tighter grip. The captain turned suddenly, and seizing the man about the waist, with an exercise of tremendous strength hurled him over his head and into the sea, the man making a great splash.

"That's the way I'll treat any one else who dares lay a hand on me!" shouted the captain, who was transformed from a mild-mannered individual into an angry, modern giant. There was a gasp of astonishment at his feat, as the ducked sailor crawled back into the small boat. And he did not again venture on the deck of the submarine.

"Seize them, men!" cried the gold-laced officer again, and this time he and his fellows, including the crew, crowded so closely around Tom and his friends that they could do nothing. Even Captain Weston found it impossible to offer any resistance, for three men grabbed hold of him.

But his spirit was still a fighting one, and he struggled desperately but uselessly.

"How dare you do this?" he cried.

"Yes," added Tom, "what right have you to interfere with us?"

"Every right," declared the gold-laced officer. "You are in Brazilian territory, and I arrest you."

"What for?" demanded Mr. Sharp.

"Because your ship is an American submarine, and we have received word that you intend to damage our shipping, and may try to torpedo our warships. I believe you tried to disable us a little while ago, but failed. We consider that an act of war and you will be treated accordingly. Take them on board the *San Paulo*," the officer went on, turning to his aides. "We'll try them by court-marital here. Some of you remain and guard this submarine. We will teach these filibustering Americans a lesson."

CHAPTER XX

DOOMED TO DEATH

THERE was no room on the small deck of the submarine to make a stand against the officers and crew of the Brazilian warship. In fact, the capture of the gold-seekers had been effected so suddenly that their astonishment almost deprived them of the power to think clearly.

At another command from the officer, who was addressed as Admiral Fanchetti, several of the sailors began to lead Tom and his friends toward the small boat.

"Do you feel all right, father?" inquired the lad anxiously, as he looked at his parent. "These scoundrels have no right to treat us so."

"Yes, Tom, I'm all right as far as the electric shock is concerned, but I don't like to be handled in this fashion."

"We ought not to submit!" burst out Mr. Damon. "Bless the stars and stripes! We ought to fight."

"There's no chance," said Mr. Sharp. "We are right under the guns of the ship. They could sink us with one shot. I guess we'll have to give in for the time being."

"It is most unpleasant, if I may be allowed the expression," commented Captain Weston mildly. He seemed to have lost his sudden anger, but there was a steely glint in his eyes, and a grim, set look around his mouth that showed his temper was kept under control only by an effort. It boded no good to the sailors who had hold of the doughty captain if he should once get loose, and it was noticed that they were on their guard.

As for Tom, he submitted quietly to the two Brazilians who had hold of either arm, and Mr. Swift was held by only one, for it was seen that he was feeble.

"Into the boat with them!" cried Admiral Fanchetti. "And guard them well, Lieutenant Drascalo, for I heard them plotting to escape," and the admiral signaled to a younger officer, who was in charge of the men guarding the prisoners.

"Lieutenant Drascalo, eh?" murmured Mr. Damon. "I think they made a mistake naming him. It ought to be Rascalo. He looks like a rascal."

"Silenceo!" exclaimed the lieutenant, scowling at the odd character.

"Bless my spark plug! He's a regular fire-eater!" went on Mr. Damon, who appeared to have fully recovered his spirits.

"Silenceo!" cried the lieutenant, scowling again, but Mr. Damon did not appear to mind.

Admiral Fanchetti and several others of the gold-laced officers remained aboard the submarine, while Tom and his friends were hustled into the small boat and rowed toward the warship.

"I hope they don't damage our craft," murmured the young inventor, as he saw the admiral enter the conning tower.

"If they do, we'll complain to the United States consul and demand damages," said Mr. Swift.

"I'm afraid we won't have a chance to communicate with the consul," remarked Captain Weston.

"What do you mean?" asked Mr. Damon. "Bless my shoelaces, but will these scoundrels——"

"Silenceo!" cried Lieutenant Drascalo quickly. "Dogs of Americans, do you wish to insult us?"

"Impossible; you wouldn't appreciate a good, genuine United States insult," murmured Tom under his breath.

"What I mean," went on the captain, "is that these people may carry the proceedings off with a high hand. You heard the admiral speak of a court-martial."

"Would they dare do that?" inquired Mr. Sharp.

"They would dare anything in this part of the world, I'm afraid," resumed Captain Weston. "I think I see their plan, though. This admiral is newly in command; his uniform shows that. He wants to make a name for himself, and he seizes on our submarine as an excuse. He can send word to his government that he destroyed a torpedo craft that sought to wreck his ship. Thus he will acquire a reputation."

"But would his government support him in such a hostile act against the United States, a friendly nation?" asked Tom.

"Oh, he would not claim to have acted against the United States as a power. He would say that it was a private submarine, and, as a matter of fact, it is. While we are under the protection of the stars and stripes, our vessel is not a Government one," and Captain Weston spoke the last in a low voice, so the scowling lieutenant could not hear.

"What will they do with us?" inquired Mr. Swift.

"Have some sort of a court-martial, perhaps," went on the captain, "and confiscate our craft.

Then they will send us back home, I expect, for they would not dare harm us."

"But take our submarine!" cried Tom. "The villains——"

"Silenceo!" shouted Lieutenant Drascalo, and he drew his sword.

By this time the small boat was under the big guns of the *San Paulo,* and the prisoners were ordered, in broken English, to mount a companion ladder that hung over the side. In a short time they were on deck, amid a crowd of sailors, and they could see the boat going back to bring off the admiral, who signaled from the submarine. Tom and his friends were taken below to a room that looked like a prison, and there, a little later, they were visited by Admiral Fanchetti and several officers.

"You will be tried at once," said the admiral. "I have examined your submarine and I find she carries two torpedo tubes. It is a wonder you did not sink me at once."

"Those are not torpedo tubes!" cried Tom, unable to keep silent, though Captain Weston motioned him to do so.

"I know torpedo tubes when I see them," declared the admiral. "I consider I had a very narrow escape. Your country is fortunate that mine does not declare war against it for this act. But I take it you are acting privately, for you fly no flag, though you claim to be from the United States."

"There's no place for a flag on the submarine," went on Tom. "What good would it be under water?"

"Silenceo!" cried Lieutenant Drascalo, the admonition to silence seeming to be the only command of which he was capable.

"I shall confiscate your craft for my government," went on the admiral, "and shall punish you as the court-martial may direct. You will be tried at once."

It was in vain for the prisoners to protest. Matters were carried with a high hand. They were allowed a spokesman, and Captain Weston, who understood Spanish, was selected, that language being used. But the defense was a farce, for he was scarcely listened to. Several officers testified before the admiral, who was judge, that they had seen the submarine rise out of the water, almost under the prow of the *San Paulo*. It was assumed that the *Advance* had tried to wreck the warship, but had failed. It was in vain that Captain Weston and the others told of the reason for their rapid ascent from the ocean depths— that Mr. Swift had been shocked, and needed fresh air. Their story was not believed.

"We have heard enough!" suddenly exclaimed the admiral. "The evidence against you is overwhelming—er—what you Americans call conclusive," and he was speaking then in broken English. "I find you guilty, and the sentence of this court-martial is that you be shot at sunrise, three days hence!"

"Shot!" cried Captain Weston, staggering back at this unexpected sentence. His companions turned white, and Mr. Swift leaned against his son for support.

"Bless my stars! Of all the scoundrelly——" began Mr. Damon.

"Silenceo!" shouted the lieutenant, waving his sword.

"You will be shot," proceeded the admiral. "Is not that the verdict of the honorable court?" he asked, looking at his fellow officers. They all nodded gravely.

"But look here!" objected Captain Weston. "You don't dare do that! We are citizens of the United States, and——"

"I consider you no better than pirates," interrupted the admiral. "You have an armed submarine—a submarine with torpedo tubes. You invade our harbor with it, and come up almost under my ship. You have forfeited your right to the protection of your country, and I have no fear on that score. You will be shot within three days. That is all. Remove the prisoners."

Protests were in vain, and it was equally useless to struggle. The prisoners were taken out on deck, for which they were thankful, for the interior of the ship was close and hot, the weather being intensely disagreeable. They were told to keep within a certain space on deck, and a guard of sailors, all armed, was placed near them. From where they were they could see their submarine floating on the surface of the little bay, with several Brazilians on the small deck. The *Advance* had been anchored, and was surrounded by a flotilla of the native boats, the brown-skinned paddlers gazing curiously at the odd craft.

"Well, this is tough luck!" murmured Tom. "How do you feel, dad?"

"As well as can be expected under the circumstances," was the reply. "What do you think about this, Captain Weston?"

"Not very much, if I may be allowed the expression," was the answer.

"Do you think they will dare carry out that threat?" asked Mr. Sharp.

The captain shrugged his shoulders. "I hope it is only a bluff," he replied, "made to scare us so we will consent to giving up the submarine, which they have no right to confiscate. But these fellows look ugly enough for anything," he went on.

"Then if there's any chance of them attempting to carry it out," spoke Tom, "we've got to do something."

"Bless my gizzard, of course!" exclaimed Mr. Damon. "But what? That's the question. To be shot! Why, that's a terrible threat! The villains——"

"Silenceo!" shouted Lieutenant Dràscalo, coming up at that moment.

CHAPTER XXI

THE ESCAPE

EVENTS had happened so quickly that day that the gold-hunters could scarcely comprehend them. It seemed only a short time since Mr. Swift had been discovered lying disabled on the dynamo, and what had transpired since seemed to have taken place in a few minutes, though it was, in reality, several hours. This was made manifest by the feeling of hunger on the part of Tom and his friends.

"I wonder if they're going to starve us, the scoundrels?" asked Mr. Sharp, when the irate lieutenant was beyond hearing. "It's not fair to make us go hungry and shoot us in the bargain."

"That's so, they ought to feed us," put in Tom. As yet neither he nor the others fully realized the meaning of the sentence passed on them.

From where they were on deck they could look off to the little island. From it boats manned by natives were constantly putting off, bringing supplies to the ship. The place appeared to be a sort of calling station for Brazilian warships, where they could get fresh water and fruit and other food.

From the island the gaze of the adventurers wandered to the submarine, which lay not far away. They were chagrined to see several of the bolder natives clambering over the deck.

"I hope they keep out of the interior," commented Tom. "If they get to pulling or hauling on the levers and wheels they may open the tanks and sink her, with the conning tower open."

"Better that, perhaps, than to have her fall into the hands of a foreign power," commented Captain Weston. "Besides, I don't see that it's going to matter much to us what becomes of her after we're——"

He did not finish, but every one knew what he meant, and a grim silence fell upon the little group.

There came a welcome diversion, however, in the shape of three sailors, bearing trays of food, which were placed on the deck in front of the prisoners, who were sitting or lying in the shade of an awning, for the sun was very hot.

"Ha! Bless my napkin-ring!" cried Mr. Damon with something of his former gaiety.

"Here's a meal, at all events. They don't intend to starve us. Eat hearty, every one."

"Yes, we need to keep up our strength," observed Captain Weston.

"Why?" inquired Mr. Sharp.

"Because we're going to try to escape!" exclaimed Tom in a low voice, when the sailors who had brought the food had gone. "Isn't that what you mean, captain?"

"Exactly. We'll try to give these villains the slip, and we'll need all our strength and wits to do it. We'll wait until night, and see what we can do."

"But where will we escape to?" asked Mr. Swift. "The island will afford no shelter, and——"

"No, but our submarine will," went on the sailor.

"It's in the possession of the Brazilians," objected Tom.

"Once I get aboard the *Advance* twenty of those brown-skinned villains won't keep me prisoner," declared Captain Weston fiercely. "If we can only slip away from here, get into the small boat, or even swim to the submarine, I'll make those chaps on board her think a hurricane has broken loose."

"Yes, and I'll help," said Mr. Damon.

"And I," added Tom and the balloonist.

"That's the way to talk," commented the captain. "Now let's eat, for I see that rascally lieutenant coming this way, and we mustn't appear to be plotting, or he'll be suspicious."

The day passed slowly, and though the prisoners seemed to be allowed considerable liberty, they soon found that it was only apparent. Once Tom walked some distance from that portion of the deck where he and the others had been told to remain. A sailor with a gun at once ordered him back. Nor could they approach the rails without being directed, harshly enough at times, to move back amidships.

As night approached the gold-seekers were on the alert for any chance that might offer to slip away, or even attack their guard, but the number of Brazilians around them was doubled in the evening, and after supper, which was served to them on deck by the light of swinging lanterns, they were taken below and locked in a stuffy cabin. They looked helplessly at each other.

"Don't give up," advised Captain Weston. "It's a long night. We may be able to get out of here."

But this hope was in vain. Several times he and Tom, thinking the guards outside the cabin were asleep, tried to force the lock of the door with their pocket-knives, which had not been taken from them. But one of the sailors was aroused each time by the noise, and looked in through a barred window, so they had to give it up. Slowly the night passed, and morning found the prisoners pale, tired and discouraged. They were brought up on deck again, for which they were thankful, as in that tropical climate it was stifling below.

During the day they saw Admiral Fanchetti and several of his officers pay a visit to the submarine. They went below through the opened conning tower, and were gone some time.

"I hope they don't disturb any of the machinery," remarked Mr. Swift. "That could easily do great damage."

Admiral Fanchetti seemed much pleased with himself when he returned from his visit to the submarine.

"You have a fine craft," he said to the prisoners. "Or, rather, you *had* one. My government now owns it. It seems a pity to shoot such good boat builders, but you are too dangerous to be allowed to go."

If there had been any doubt in the minds of Tom and his friends that the sentence of the court-martial was only for effect, it was dispelled that day. A firing squad was told off in plain view of them, and the men were put through their evolutions by Lieutenant Drascalo, who had them load, aim and fire blank cartridges at an imaginary line of prisoners. Tom could not repress a shudder as he noted the leveled rifles, and saw the fire and smoke spurt from the muzzles.

"Thus we shall do to you at sunrise to-morrow," said the lieutenant, grinning, as he once more had his men practice their grim work.

It seemed hotter than ever that day. The sun was fairly broiling, and there was a curious haziness and stillness to the air. It was noticed that the sailors on the *San Paulo* were busy making fast all loose articles on deck with extra lashings, and hatch coverings were doubly secured.

"What do you suppose they are up to?" asked Tom of Captain Weston.

"I think it is coming on to blow," he replied, "and they don't want to be caught napping. They have fearful storms down in this region at this season of the year, and I think one is about due."

"I hope it doesn't wreck the submarine," spoke Mr. Swift. "They ought to close the hatch of the conning tower, for it won't take much of a sea to make her ship considerable water."

Admiral Fanchetti had thought of this, however, and as the afternoon wore away and the storm signs multiplied, he sent word to close the submarine. He left a few sailors aboard inside on guard.

"It's too hot to eat," observed Tom, when their supper had been brought to them, and the others felt the same way about it. They managed to drink some cocoanut milk, prepared in a palatable fashion by the natives of the island, and then, much to their disgust, they were taken below again and locked in the cabin.

"Whew! But it certainly is hot!" exclaimed Mr. Damon as he sat down on a couch and fanned himself. "This is awful!"

"Yes, something is going to happen pretty soon," observed Captain Weston. "The storm will break shortly, I think."

They sat languidly about the cabin. It was so oppressive that even the thought of the doom that awaited them in the morning could hardly seem worse than the terrible heat. They could hear movements going on about the ship, movements which indicated that preparations were being made for something unusual. There was a rattling of a chain through a hawse hole, and Captain Weston remarked:

"They're putting down another anchor. Admiral Fanchetti had better get away from the island, though, unless he wants to be wrecked. He'll be blown ashore in less than no time. No cable or chain will hold in such storms as they have here."

There came a period of silence, which was suddenly broken by a howl as of some wild beast.

"What's that?" cried Tom, springing up from where he was stretched out on the cabin floor.

"Only the wind," replied the captain. "The storm has arrived."

The howling kept up, and soon the ship began to rock. The wind increased, and a little later there could be heard, through an opened port in the prisoners' cabin, the dash of rain.

"It's a regular hurricane!" exclaimed the captain. "I wonder if the cables will hold?"

"What about the submarine?" asked Mr. Swift anxiously.

"I haven't much fear for her. She lies so low in the water that the wind can't get much hold on her. I don't believe she'll drag her anchor."

Once more came a fierce burst of wind, and a dash of rain, and then, suddenly above the outburst of the elements, there sounded a crash on deck. It was followed by excited cries.

"Something's happened!" yelled Tom. The prisoners gathered in a frightened group in the middle of the cabin. The cries were repeated, and then came a rush of feet just outside the cabin door.

"Our guards! They're leaving!" shouted Tom.

"Right!" exclaimed Captain Weston. "Now's our chance! Come on! If we're going to escape we must do it while the storm is at its height, and all is in confusion. Come on!"

Tom tried the door. It was locked.

"One side!" shouted the captain, and this time he did not pause to say "by your leave." He came at the portal on the run, and his shoulder struck it squarely. There was a splintering and crashing of wood, and the door was burst open.

"Follow me!" cried the valiant sailor, and Tom and the others rushed after him. They could hear the wind howling more loudly than ever, and as they reached the deck the rain dashed into their faces with such violence that they could hardly see. But they were aware that something had occurred. By the light of several lanterns swaying in the terrific blast they saw that one of the auxiliary masts had broken off near the deck.

It had fallen against the chart house, smashing it, and a number of sailors were laboring to clear away the wreckage.

"Fortune favors us!" cried Captain Weston. "Come on! Make for the small boat. It's near the side ladder. We'll lower the boat and pull to the submarine."

There came a flash of lightning, and in its glare Tom saw something that caused him to cry out.

"Look!" he shouted. "The submarine. She's dragged her anchors!"

The *Advance* was much closer to the warship than she had been that afternoon. Captain Weston looked over the side.

"It's the *San Paulo* that's dragging her anchors, not the submarine!" he shouted. "We're bearing down on her! We must act quickly. Come on, we'll lower the boat!"

In the rush of wind and the dash of rain the prisoners crowded to the accommodation companion ladder, which was still over the side of the big ship. No one seemed to be noticing them, for Admiral Fanchetti was on the bridge, yelling orders for the clearing away of the wreckage. But Lieutenant Drascalo, coming up from below at that moment, caught sight of the fleeing ones. Drawing his sword, he rushed at them, shouting:

"The prisoners! The prisoners! They are escaping!"

Captain Weston leaped toward the lieutenant.

"Look out for his sword!" cried Tom. But the doughty sailor did not fear the weapon. Catching up a coil of rope, he cast it at the lieutenant. It struck him in the chest, and he staggered back, lowering his sword.

Captain Weston leaped forward, and with a terrific blow sent Lieutenant Drascalo to the deck.

"There!" cried the sailor. "I guess you won't yell 'Silenceo!' for a while now."

There was a rush of Brazilians toward the group of prisoners. Tom caught one with a blow on the chin, and felled him, while Captain Weston disposed of two more, and Mr. Sharp and Mr. Damon one each. The savage fighting of the Americans was too much for the foreigners, and they drew back.

"Come on!" cried Captain Weston again. "The storm is getting worse. The warship will crash into the submarine in a few minutes. Her anchors aren't holding. I didn't think they would."

He made a dash for the ladder, and a glance showed him that the small boat was in the water at the foot of it. The craft had not been hoisted on the davits.

"Luck's with us at last!" cried Tom, seeing it also. "Shall I help you, dad?"

"No; I think I'm all right. Go ahead."

There came such a gust of wind that the *San Paulo* was heeled over, and the wreck of the mast, rolling about, crashed into the side of a deck house, splintering it. A crowd of sailors, led by Admiral Fanchetti, who were again rushing on the escaping prisoners, had to leap back out of the way of the rolling mast.

"Catch them! Don't let them get away!" begged the commander, but the sailors evidently had no desire to close in with the Americans.

Through the rush of wind and rain Tom and his friends staggered down the ladder. It was hard work to maintain one's footing, but they managed it. On account of the high side of the ship the water was comparatively calm under her lee, and, though the small boat was bobbing about, they got aboard. The oars were in place, and in another moment they had shoved off from the landing stage which formed the foot of the accommodation ladder.

"Now for the *Advance!*" murmured Captain Weston.

"Come back! Come back, dogs of Americans!" cried a voice at the rail over their heads, and looking up, Tom saw Lieutenant Drascalo. He had snatched a carbine from a marine, and was pointing it at the recent prisoners. He fired, the flash of the gun and a dazzling chain of lightning coming together. The thunder swallowed up the report of the carbine, but the bullet whistled uncomfortable close to Tom's head. The blackness that followed the lightning shut out the view of everything for a few seconds, and when the next flash came the adventurers saw that they were close to their submarine.

A fusilade of shots sounded from the deck of the warship, but as the marines were poor marksmen at best, and as the swaying of the ship disconcerted them, our friends were in little danger.

There was quite a sea once they were beyond the protection of the side of the warship, but Captain Weston, who was rowing, knew how to manage a boat skilfully, and he soon had the craft alongside the bobbing submarine.

"Get aboard, now, quick!" he cried.

They leaped to the small deck, casting the rowboat adrift. It was the work of but a moment to open the conning tower. As they started to descend they were met by several Brizilians coming up.

"Overboard with 'em!" yelled the captain. "Let them swim ashore or to their ship!"

With almost superhuman strength he tossed one big sailor from the small deck. Another showed fight, but he went to join his companion in the swirling water. A man rushed at Tom, seeking the while to draw his sword, but the young inventor, with a neat left-hander, sent him to join the other two, and the remainder did not wait to try conclusions. They leaped for their lives, and soon all could be seen, in the frequent lightning flashes, swimming toward the warship, which was now closer than ever to the submarine.

"Get inside and we'll sink below the surface!" called Tom. "Then we don't care what happens."

They closed the steel door of the conning tower. As they did so they heard the patter of bullets from carbines fired from the *San Paulo*. Then came a violent tossing of the *Advance;* the waves were becoming higher as they caught the full force of the hurricane. It took but an instant to sever, from within, the cable attached to the anchor, which was one belonging to the warship. The *Advance* began drifting.

"Open the tanks, Mr. Sharp!" cried Tom. "Captain Weston and I will steer. Once below we'll start the engines."

Amid a crash of thunder and dazzling flashes of lightning, the submarine began to sink. Tom, in the conning tower had a sight of the *San Paulo* as it drifted nearer and nearer under the influence of the mighty wind. As one bright flash came he saw Admiral Fanchetti and Lieutenant Drascalo leaning over the rail and gazing at the *Advance*.

A moment later the view faded from sight as the submarine sank below the surface of the troubled sea. She was tossed about for some time until deep enough to escape the surface motion. Waiting until she was far enough down so that her lights would not offer a mark for the guns of the warship, the electrics were switched on.

"We're safe now!" cried Tom, helping his father to his cabin. "They've got too much to attend to themselves to follow us now, even if they could. Shall we go ahead, Captain Weston?"

"I think so, yes, if I may be allowed to express my opinion," was the mild reply, in strange contrast to the strenuous work in which the captain had just been engaged.

Tom signaled to Mr. Sharp in the engine-room, and in a few seconds the *Advance* was speeding away from the island and the hostile vessel. Nor, deep as she was now, was there any sign of the hurricane. In the peaceful depths she was once more speeding toward the sunken treasure.

CHAPTER XXII

AT THE WRECK

"Well," remarked Mr. Damon, as the submarine hurled herself forward through the ocean, "I guess that firing party will have something else to do to-morrow morning besides aiming those rifles at us."

"Yes, indeed," agreed Tom. "They'll be lucky if they save their ship. My, how that wind did blow!"

"You're right," put in Captain Weston. "When they get a hurricane down in this region it's no cat's paw. But they were a mighty careless lot of sailors. The idea of leaving the ladder over the side, and the boat in the water."

"It was a good thing for us, though," was Tom's opinion.

"Indeed it was," came from the captain. "But as long as we are safe now I think we'd better take a look about the craft to see if those chaps did any damage. They can't have done much, though, or she wouldn't be running so smoothly. Suppose you go take a look, Tom, and ask your father and Mr. Sharp what they think. I'll steer for a while, until we get well away from the island."

The young inventor found his father and the balloonist busy in the engine-room. Mr. Swift had already begun an inspection of the machinery, and so far found that it had not been injured. A further inspection showed that no damage had been done by the foreign guard that had been in temporary possession of the *Advance,* though the sailors had made free in the cabins, and had broken into the food lockers, helping themselves plentifully. But there was still enough for the gold-seekers.

"You'd never know there was a storm raging up above," observed Tom as he rejoined Captain Weston in the lower pilot house, where he was managing the craft. "It's as still and peaceful here as one could wish."

"Yes, the extreme depths are seldom disturbed by a surface storm. But we are over a mile deep now. I sent her down a little while you were gone, as I think she rides a little more steadily.

All that night they speeded forward, and the next day, rising to the surface to take an observation, they found no traces of the storm, which had blown itself out. They were several hundred miles away from the hostile warship, and there was not a vessel in sight on the broad expanse of blue ocean.

The air tanks were refilled, and after sailing along on the surface for an hour or two, the submarine was again sent below, as Captain Weston sighted through his telescope the smoke of a distant steamer.

"As long as it isn't the *Wonder,* we're all right," said Tom. "Still, we don't want to answer a lot of questions about ourselves and our object."

"No. I fancy the *Wonder* will give up the search," remarked the captain, as the *Advance* was sinking to the depths.

"We must be getting pretty near to the end of our search ourselves," ventured the young inventor.

"We are within five hundred miles of the intersection of the forty-fifth parallel and the twenty-seventh meridian, east from Washington," said the captain. "That's as near as I could locate the wreck. Once we reach that point we will have to search about under water, for I don't fancy the other divers left any buoys to mark the spot."

It was two days later, after uneventful sailing, partly on the surface, and partly submerged, that

Captain Weston, taking a noon observation, announced:

"Well, we're here!"

"Do you mean at the wreck?" asked Mr. Swift eagerly.

"We're at the place where she is supposed to lie, in about two miles of water," replied the captain. "We are quite a distance off the coast of Uruguay, about opposite the harbor of Rio de La Plata. From now on we shall have to nose about under water, and trust to luck."

With her air tanks filled to their capacity, and Tom having seen that the oxygen machine and other apparatus was in perfect working order, the submarine was sent below on her search. Though they were in the neighborhood of the wreck, the adventurers might still have to do considerable searching before locating it. Lower and lower they sank into the depths of the sea, down and down, until they were deeper than they had ever gone before. The pressure was tremendous, but the steel sides of the *Advance* withstood it.

Then began a search that lasted nearly a week. Back and forth they cruised, around in great circles, with the powerful searchlight focused to disclose the sunken treasure ship. Once Tom, who was observing the path of light in the depths from the conning tower, thought he had seen the

remains of the *Boldero,* for a misty shape loomed
up in front of the submarine, and he signaled for
a quick stop. It was a wreck, but it had been
on the ocean bed for a score of years, and only
a few timbers remained of what had been a great
ship. Much disappointed, Tom rang for full
speed ahead again, and the current was sent into
the great electric plates that pulled and pushed the
submarine forward.

For two days more nothing happened. They
searched around under the green waters, on the
alert for the first sign, but they saw nothing.
Great fish swam about them, sometimes racing
with the *Advance.* The adventurers beheld great
ocean caverns, and skirted immense rocks, where
dwelt monsters of the deep. Once a great octupus
tried to do battle with the submarine and crush it
in its snaky arms, but Tom saw the great white
body, with saucer-shaped eyes, in the path of light
and rammed him with the steel point. The creature died after a struggle.

They were beginning to despair when a full
week had passed and they were seemingly as far
from the wreck as ever. They went to the surface to enable Captain Weston to take another
observation. It only confirmed the other, and
showed that they were in the right vicinity. But
it was like looking for a needle in a haystack,

almost, to find the sunken ship in that depth of water.

"Well, we'll try again," said Mr. Swift, as they sank once more beneath the surface.

It was toward evening, on the second day after this, that Tom, who was on duty in the conning tower, saw a black shape looming up in front of the submarine, the searchlight revealing it to him far enough away so that he could steer to avoid it. He thought at first that it was a great rock, for they were moving along near the bottom, but the peculiar shape of it soon convinced him that this could not be. It came more plainly into view as the submarine approached it more slowly, then suddenly, out of the depths in the illumination from the searchlight, the young inventor saw the steel sides of a steamer. His heart gave a great thump, but he would not call out yet, fearing that it might be some other vessel than the one containing the treasure.

He steered the *Advance* so as to circle it. As he swept past the bows he saw in big letters near the sharp prow the word, *Boldero*.

"The wreck! The wreck!" he cried, his voice ringing through the craft from end to end. "We've found the wreck at last!"

"Are you sure?" cried his father, hurrying to his son, Captain Weston following.

"Positive," answered the lad. The submarine was slowing up now, and Tom sent her around on the other side. They had a good view of the sunken ship. It seemed to be intact, no gaping holes in her sides, for only her plates had started, allowing her to sink gradually.

"At last," murmured Mr. Swift. "Can it be possible we are about to get the treasure?"

"That's the *Boldero,* all right," affirmed Captain Weston. "I recognize her, even if the name wasn't on her bow. Go right down on the bottom, Tom, and we'll get out the diving suits and make an examination."

The submarine settled to the ocean bed. Tom glanced at the depth gage. It showed over two miles and a half. Would they be able to venture out into water of such enormous pressure in the comparatively frail diving suits, and wrest the gold from the wreck? It was a serious question.

The *Advance* came to a stop. In front of her loomed the great bulk of the *Boldero,* vague and shadowy in the flickering gleam of the searchlight. As the gold-seekers looked at her through the bull's-eyes of the conning tower, several great forms emerged from beneath the wreck's bows.

"Deep-water sharks!" exclaimed Captain Weston, "and monsters, too. But they can't bother us. Now to get out the gold!"

CHAPTER XXIII

ATTACKED BY SHARKS

FOR a few minutes after reaching the wreck, which had so occupied their thoughts for the past weeks, the adventurers did nothing but gaze at it from the ports of the submarine. The appearance of the deep-water sharks gave them no concern, for they did not imagine the ugly creatures would attack them. The treasure-seekers were more engrossed with the problem of getting out the gold.

"How are we going to get at it?" asked Tom, as he looked at the high sides of the sunken ship, which towered well above the comparatively small *Advance*.

"Why, just go in and get it," suggested Mr. Damon. "Where is gold in a cargo usually kept, Captain Weston? You ought to know, I should think. Bless my pocketbook!"

"Well, I should say that in this case the bullion would be kept in a safe in the captain's cabin," replied the sailor. "Or, if not there, in some after part of the vessel, away from where the crew is quartered. But it is going to be quite a problem to get at it. We can't climb the sides of the wreck, and it will be impossible to lower her ladder over the side. However, I think we had better get into the diving suits and take a closer look. We can walk around her."

"That's my idea," put in Mr. Sharp. "But who will go, and who will stay with the ship?"

"I think Tom and Captain Weston had better go," suggested Mr. Swift. "Then, in case anything happens, Mr. Sharp, you and I will be on board to manage matters."

"You don't think anything will happen, do you, dad?" asked his son with a laugh, but it was not an easy one, for the lad was thinking of the shadowy forms of the ugly sharks.

"Oh, no, but it's best to be prepared," answered his father.

The captain and the young inventor lost no time in donning the diving suits. They each took a heavy metal bar, pointed at one end, to use in assisting them to walk on the bed of the ocean, and as a protection in case the sharks might attack them. Entering the diving chamber, they were shut in, and then water was admitted until the pressure was seen, by gages, to be the same as that

outside the submarine. Then the sliding steel
door was opened. At first Tom and the captain
could barely move, so great was the pressure of
water on their bodies. They would have been
crushed but for the protection afforded by the
strong diving suits.

In a few minutes they became used to it, and
stepped out on the floor of the ocean. They could
not, of course, speak to each other, but Tom
looked through the glass eyes of his helmet at
the captain, and the latter motioned for the lad
to follow. The two divers could breathe perfectly, and by means of small, but powerful lights on
the helmets, the way was lighted for them as they
advanced.

Slowly they approached the wreck, and began
a circuit of her. They could see several places
where the pressure of the water, and the strain
of the storm in which she had foundered, had
opened the plates of the ship, but in no case were
the openings large enough to admit a person.
Captain Weston put his steel bar in one crack,
and tried to pry it farther open, but his strength
was not equal to the task. He made some peculiar motions, but Tom could not understand
them.

They looked for some means by which they
could mount to the decks of the *Boldero,* but none

was visible. It was like trying to scale a fifty-foot smooth steel wall. There was no place for a foothold. Again the sailor made some peculiar motions, and the lad puzzled over them. They had gone nearly around the wreck now, and as yet had seen no way in which to get at the gold. As they passed around the bow, which was in a deep shadow from a great rock, they caught sight of the submarine lying a short distance away. Light streamed from many bull's-eyes, and Tom felt a sense of security as he looked at her, for it was lonesome enough in that great depth of water, unable to speak to his companion, who was a few feet in advance.

Suddenly there was a swirling of the water, and Tom was nearly thrown off his feet by the rush of some great body. A long, black shadow passed over his head, and an instant later he saw the form of a great shark launched at Captain Weston. The lad involuntarily cried in alarm, but the result was surprising. He was nearly deafened by his own voice, confined as the sound was in the helmet he wore. But the sailor, too, had felt the movement of the water, and turned just in time. He thrust upward with his pointed bar. But he missed the stroke, and Tom, a moment later, saw the great fish turn over so that its mouth, which is far underneath its snout, could take in the queer shape which the shark evidently thought was a choice morsel. The big fish did actually get the helmet of Captain Weston inside its jaws, but probably it would have found it impossible to crush the strong steel. Still it might have sprung the joints, and water would have entered, which would have been as fatal as though the sailor had been swallowed by the shark. Tom realized this and, moving as fast as he could through the water, he came up behind the monster and drove his steel bar deep into it.

The sea was crimsoned with blood, and the savage creature, opening its mouth, let go of the captain. It turned on Tom, who again harpooned it. Then the fish darted off and began a wild flurry, for it was dying. The rush of water nearly threw Tom off his feet, but he managed to make his way over to his friend, and assist him to rise. A confident look from the sailor showed the lad that Captain Weston was uninjured, though he must have been frightened. As the two turned to make their way back to the submarine, the waters about them seemed alive with the horrible monsters.

It needed but a glance to show what they were. Sharks! Scores of them, long, black ones, with their ugly, undershot mouths. They had been attracted by the blood of the one Tom had killed, but there was not a meal for all of them off the dying creature, and the great fish might turn on the young inventor and his companion.

The two shrank closer toward the wreck. They might get under the prow of that and be safe. But even as they started to move, several of the sea wolves darted quickly at them. Tom glanced at the captain. What could they do? Strong as were the diving suits, a combined attack by the sharks, with their powerful jaws, would do untold damage.

At that moment there seemed some movement on board the submarine. Tom could see his father looking from the conning tower, and the aged inventor seemed to be making some motions. Then Tom understood. Mr. Swift was directing his son and Captain Weston to crouch down. The lad did so, pulling the sailor after him. Then Tom saw the bow electric gun run out, and aimed at the mass of sharks, most of whom were congregated about the dead one. Into the midst of the monsters was fired a number of small projectiles, which could be used in the electric cannon in place of the solid shot. Once more the waters were red with blood, and those sharks which were not killed swirled off. Tom and Captain Weston were saved. They were soon inside the submarine again, telling their thrilling story.

"It's lucky you saw us, dad," remarked the lad, blushing at the praise Mr. Damon bestowed on him for killing the monster which had attacked the captain.

"Oh, I was on the lookout," said the inventor. "But what about getting into the wreck?"

"I think the only way we can do it will be to ram a hole in her side," said Captain Weston. "That was what I tried to tell Tom by motions, but he didn't seem to understand me."

"No," replied the lad, who was still a little nervous from his recent experience. "I thought you meant for us to turn it over, bottom side up," and he laughed.

"Bless my gizzard! Just like a shark," commented Mr. Damon.

"Please don't mention them," begged Tom. "I hope we don't see any more of them."

"Oh, I fancy they have been driven far enough away from this neighborhood now," commented the captain. "But now about the wreck. We may be able to approach it from above. Suppose we try to lower the submarine on it? That will save ripping it open."

This was tried a little later, but would not work. There were strong currents sweeping over the top of the *Boldero,* caused by a submerged reef near which she had settled. It was a delicate task to sink the submarine on her decks, and with the deep waters swirling about was found to be impossible, even with the use of the electric plates and the auxiliary screws. Once more the *Advance* settled to the ocean bed, near the wreck.

"Well, what's to be done?" asked Tom, as he looked at the high steel sides.

"Ram her, tear a hole, and then use dynamite," decided Captain Weston promptly. "You have some explosive, haven't you, Mr. Swift?"

"Oh, yes. I came prepared for emergencies."

"Then we'll blow up the wreck and get at the gold."

CHAPTER XXIV

RAMMING THE WRECK

FITTED with a long, sharp steel ram in front, the *Advance* was peculiarly adapted for this sort of work. In designing the ship this ram was calculated to be used against hostile vessels in war time, for the submarine was at first, as we know, destined for a Government boat. Now the ram was to serve a good turn.

To make sure that the attempt would be a success, the machinery of the craft was carefully gone over. It was found to be in perfect order, save for a few adjustments which were needed. Then, as it was night, though there was no difference in the appearance of things below the surface, it was decided to turn in, and begin work in the morning. Nor did the gold-seekers go to the surface, for they feared they might encounter a storm.

"We had trouble enough locating the wreck," said Captain Weston, "and if we go up we may be blown off our course. We have air enough to stay below, haven't we, Tom?"

"Plenty," answered the lad, looking at the gages.

After a hearty breakfast the next morning, the submarine crew got ready for their hard task. The craft was backed away as far as was practical, and then, running at full speed, she rammed the wreck. The shock was terrific, and at first it was feared some damage had been done to the *Advance,* but she stood the strain.

"Did we open up much of a hole?" anxiously asked Mr. Swift.

"Pretty good," replied Tom, observing it through the conning tower bull's-eyes, when the submarine had backed off again. "Let's give her another."

Once more the great steel ram hit into the side of the *Boldero,* and again the submarine shivered from the shock. But there was a bigger hole in the wreck now, and after Captain Weston had viewed it he decided it was large enough to allow a person to enter and place a charge of dynamite so that the treasure ship would be broken up.

Tom and the captain placed the explosive. Then the *Advance* was withdrawn to a safe distance. There was a dull rumble, a great swirling of the water, which was made murky; but when it cleared, and the submarine went back, it was seen that the wreck was effectively broken up. It was in two parts, each one easy of access.

"That's the stuff!" cried Tom. "Now to get at the gold!"

"Yes, get out the diving suits," added Mr. Damon. "Bless my watch-charm, I think I'll chance it in one myself! Do you think the sharks are all gone, Caiptain Weston?"

"I think so."

In a short time Tom, the captain, Mr. Sharp and Mr. Damon were attired in the diving suits, Mr. Swift not caring to venture into such a great depth of water. Besides, it was necessary for at least one person to remain in the submarine to operate the diving chamber.

Walking slowly along the bottom of the sea, the four gold-seekers approached the wreck. They looked on all sides for a sight of the sharks, but the monster fish seemed to have deserted that part of the ocean. Tom was the first to reach the now disrupted steamer. He found he could easily climb up, for boxes and barrels from the cargo holds were scattered all about by the explosion. Captain Weston soon joined the lad. The sailor motioned Tom to follow him, and being more familiar with ocean craft the captain was permitted to take the lead. He headed aft, seeking to locate

the captain's cabin. Nor was he long in finding
it. He motioned for the others to enter, that the
combined illumination of the lamps in their
helmets would make the place bright enough so a
search could be made for the gold. Tom suddenly seized the arm of the captain, and pointed
to one corner of the cabin. There stood a small
safe, and at the sight of it Captain Weston moved
toward it. The door was not locked, probably
having been left open when the ship was deserted.
Swinging it back the interior was revealed.

It was empty. There was no gold bullion in it.

There was no mistaking the dejected air of
Captain Weston. The others shared his feelings,
but though they all felt like voicing their disap-
pointment, not a word could be spoken. Mr.
Sharp, by vigorous motions, indicated to his companions to seek further.

They did so, spending all the rest of the day
in the wreck, save for a short interval for dinner.
But no gold rewarded their search.

Tom, late that afternoon, wandered away from
the others, and found himself in the captain's
cabin again, with the empty safe showing dimly
in the water that was all about.

"Hang it all!" thought the lad, "we've had all
our trouble for nothing!" They must have taken
the gold with them."

Idly he raised his steel bar, and struck it against the partition back of the safe. To his astonishment the partition seemed to fall inward, revealing a secret compartment. The lad leaned forward to bring the light for his helmet to play on the recess. He saw a number of boxes, piled one upon the other. He had accidentally touched a hidden spring and opened a secret receptacle. But what did it contain?

Tom reached in and tried to lift one of the boxes. He found it beyond his strength. Trembling from excitement, he went in search of the others. He found them delving in the after part of the wreck, but by motions our hero caused them to follow him. Captain Weston showed the excitement he felt as soon as he caught sight of the boxes. He and Mr. Sharp lifted one out, and placed it on the cabin floor. They pried off the top with their bars.

There, packed in layers, were small yellow bars; dull, gleaming, yellow bars! It needed but a glance to show that they were gold bullion. Tom had found the treasure. The lad tried to dance around there in the cabin of the wreck, nearly three miles below the surface of the ocean, but the pressure of water was too much for him. Their trip had been successful.

CHAPTER XXV.

HOME WITH THE GOLD

THERE was no time to be lost. They were in a treacherous part of the ocean, and strong currents might at any time further break up the wreck, so that they could not come at the gold. It was decided, by means of motions, to at once transfer the treasure to the submarine. As the boxes were too heavy to carry easily, especially as two men, who were required to lift one, could not walk together in the uncertain footing afforded by the wreck, another plan was adopted. The boxes were opened and the bars, a few at a time, were dropped on a firm, sandy place at the side of the wreck. Tom and Captain Weston did this work, while Mr. Sharp and Mr. Damon carried the bullion to the diving chamber of the *Advance*. They put the yellow bars inside, and when quite a number had been thus shifted, Mr. Swift, closing the chamber, pumped the water out and removed the gold. Then he opened the chamber to the divers again, and the process was repeated, until all the bullion had been secured.

Tom would have been glad to make a further examination of the wreck, for he thought he could get some of the rifles the ship carried, but Captain Weston signed to him not to attempt this.

The lad went to the pilot house, while his father and Mr. Sharp took their places in the engine-room. The gold had been safely stowed in Mr. Swift's cabin.

Tom took a last look at the wreck before he gave the starting signal. As he gazed at the bent and twisted mass of steel that had once been a great ship, he saw something long, black and shadowy moving around from the other side, coming across the bows.

"There's another big shark," he observed to Captain Weston. "They're coming back after us."

The captain did not speak. He was staring at the dark form. Suddenly, from what seemed the pointed nose of it, there gleamed a light, as from some great eye.

"Look at that!" cried Tom. "That's no shark!"

"If you want my opinion," remarked the sailor, "I should say it was the other submarine—that of Berg and his friends—the *Wonder*. They've managed to fix up their craft and are after the gold."

"But they're too late!" cried Tom excitedly. "Let's tell them so."

"No, advised the captain. "We don't want any trouble with them."

Mr. Swift came forward to see why his son had not given the signal to start. He was shown the other submarine, for now that the *Wonder* had turned on several searchlights, there was no doubt as to the identity of the craft.

"Let's get away unobserved if we can," he suggested. "We have had trouble enough."

It was easy to do this, as the *Advance* was hidden behind the wreck, and her lights were glowing but dimly. Then, too, those in the other submarine were so excited over the finding of what they supposed was the wreck containing the treasure, that they paid little attention to anything else.

"I wonder how they'll feel when they find the gold gone?" asked Tom as he pulled the lever starting the pumps.

"Well, we may have a chance to learn, when we get back to civilization," remarked the captain.

The surface was soon reached, and then, under fair skies, and on a calm sea, the voyage home was begun. Part of the time the *Advance* sailed on the top, and part of the time submerged.

They met with but a single accident, and that was when the forward electrical plate broke. But with the aft one still in commission, and the auxiliary screws, they made good time. Just before reaching home they settled down to the bottom and donned the diving suits again, even Mr. Swift taking his turn. Mr. Damon caught some large lobsters, of which he was very fond, or, rather, to be more correct, the lobsters caught him. When he entered the diving chamber there were four fine ones clinging to different parts of his diving suit. Some of them were served for dinner.

The adventurers safely reached the New Jersey coast, and the submarine was docked. Mr. Swift at once communicated with the proper authorities concerning the recovery of the gold. He offered to divide with the actual owners, after he and his friends had been paid for their services, but as the revolutionary party to whom the bullion was intended had gone out of existence, there was no one to officially claim the treasure, so it all went to Tom and his friends, who made an equitable distribution of it. The young inventor did not forget to buy Mrs. Baggert a fine diamond ring, as he had promised.

As for Berg and his employers, they were, it

was learned later, greatly chagrined at finding
the wreck valueless. They tried to make trouble
for Tom and his father, but were not successful.

A few days after arriving at the seacoast cottage, Tom, his father and Mr. Damon went to
Shopton in the airship. Captain Weston, Garret
Jackson and Mr. Sharp remained behind in charge
of the submarine. It was decided that the Swifts
would keep the craft and not sell it to the Govern-
men, as Tom said they might want to go after
more treasure some day.

"I must first deposit this gold," said Mr. Swift
as the airship landed in front of the shed at his
home. "It won't do to keep it in the house over
night, even if the Happy Harry gang is in jail."

Tom helped him take it to the bank. As they
were making perhaps the largest single deposit
ever put in the institution, Ned Newton came out.

"Well, Tom," he cried to his chum, "it seems
that you are never going to stop doing things.
You've conquered the air, the earth and the
water."

"What have you been doing while I've been
under water, Ned?" asked the young inventor.

"Oh, the same old thing. Running errands and
doing all sorts of work in the bank."

Tom had a sudden idea. He whispered to his
father and Mr. Swift nodded. A little later he

was closeted with Mr. Prendergast, the bank president. It was not long before Ned and Tom were called in.

"I have some good news for you, Ned," said Mr. Prendergast, while Tom smiled. "Mr. Swift, er—ahem—one of our largest depositors, has spoken to me about you, Ned. I find that you have been very faithful. You are hereby appointed assistant cashier, and of course you will get a much larger salary."

Ned could hardly believe it, but he knew then what Tom had whispered to Mr. Swift. The wishes of a depositor who brings much gold bullion to a bank can hardly be ignored.

"Come on out and have some soda," invited Tom, and when Ned looked inquiringly at the president, the latter nodded an assent.

As the two lads were crossing the street to a drug store, something whizzed past them, nearly running them down.

"What sort of an auto was that?" cried Tom.

"That? Oh, that was Andy Foger's new car," answered Ned. "He's been breaking the speed laws every day lately, but no one seems to bother him. It's because his father is rich, I suppose. Andy says he has the fastest car ever built."

"He has, eh?" remarked Tom, while a curious

look came into his eyes. "Well, maybe I can build one that will beat his."

And whether the young inventor did or not you can learn by reading the fifth volume of this series, to be called "Tom Swift and His Electric Runabout; Or, The Speediest Car on the Road."

"Well, Tom, I certainly appreciate what you did for me in getting me a better position," remarked Ned as they left the drug store. "I was beginning to think I'd never get promoted. Say, have you anything to do this evening? If you haven't, I wish you'd come over to my house. I've got a lot of pictures I took while you were away."

"Sorry, but I can't," replied Tom.

"Why, are you going to build another airship or submarine?"

"No, but I'm going to see—— Oh, what do you want to know for, anyhow?" demanded the young inventor with a blush. "Can't a fellow go see a girl without being cross-questioned?"

"Oh, of course," replied Ned with a laugh. "Give Miss Nestor my regards," and at this Tom blushed still more. But, as he said, that was his own affair.

THE END